THE X-LIST

LARSSON SIBLINGS SERIES
BOOK 3

EVIE MITCHELL

THUNDER THIGHS PUBLISHING

This book is a work of fiction. Names, characters, places, incidents, facts, and sometimes random sentences are either the product of the author's imagination or are used in what she hopes is an entirely flattering but fictitious manner. Any resemblance to actual persons, living or dead, or actual events, or locales is entirely coincidental.

Editors: Nicole Wilson, Evermore Editing
http://www.evermoreediting.wixsite.com/info
Illustrator: Laras Putri

ACKNOWLEDGEMENT OF COUNTRY

I acknowledge the Traditional Custodians of the lands on which I write, the Ngunnawal people, and pay my respect to elders both past and present.

I acknowledge the continued and deep spiritual relationship of the Australian Aboriginal and Torres Strait Islander peoples' to this land, and their unique cultural and spiritual relationships to the land, waters and seas and their rich contribution to society.

Always was, always will be.

This book contains graphic and explicit descriptions of sex. The book includes references to overcoming body image struggles, and learning to love your own skin.

The main female character was born with a limb difference and uses a prosthetic. She is also a foster child, and discusses her experiences and the value of found family.

The male main character is a virgin. He is also the youngest in his family and references difficult relationships with family.

While all care has been taken to ensure representation is respectful and inclusive, my sensitivity readers and my personal experience is limited to our own knowledge and understanding. If there is anything in the book that raises concerns for you, please feel free to reach out to EvieMitchellAuthor@gmail.com.

To anyone who ever assumed you were unlovable.
Fuck that!
You're a badass, loveable, amazing human.
KNOW YOUR WORTH!

And to my husband, who made me watch Naked and Afraid in exchange for him reading three romance novels.
Jokes on you, Pal. I LOVED the series, and got some great D.
#WifeWin

I'd also like to acknowledge my awesome sensitivity readers for all their feedback on Gabby's disability.
She's a badass thanks to them!

THE X-LIST

Rune

What kind of crazy person doesn't read? Apparently, my new neighbor. She's loud, sassy, flirty and infuriatingly, annoyingly cheerful.

And a non-reader. The worst kind of human.

So why is that when I dare her to enter the charity read-a-thon, I suddenly find myself carefully curating her list?

And those books... they're not your momma's romance.

Gabby

I'm used to people underestimating me. Normally I can brush it off with a laugh. But Rune? He gets under my skin.

So when he makes an off-handed comment
that a non-reader like me shouldn't bother with
the town's charity event, I can't help but accept
the challenge.

Only these books are not what I remember
from the school book list. Not. Even. Close.

And Rune? Well, I'm beginning to see him
in a new light.

Or, should I say, hear him?

*Warning: This hot little number is inspired by
hot books, men who read, and a slight
exhibitionist kink. Get thee a man who knows
how to handle you between the covers, and settle
in — this enemies-to-lovers will have you
begging for more.*

CHAPTER 1

Gabby

"We're here," I whispered to myself as I pulled up behind the moving van, parking my car in front of the gorgeous duplex bungalow. A thrill of excitement ratcheted down my spine, sending the butterflies in my stomach fluttering with nervous anticipation.

Gunnar, my boss, came from around the front of the truck, giving me a smile. I exited my car, coming to meet him halfway.

"Welcome to Cape Hardgrave," he gestured at the bungalow. "Not much to look at on the outside, but she'll do for the next six months."

The bungalow was a single level brick and

weatherboard home. It looked as if it were an original build, but had been divided up and updated at some point over the last fifty years. Whoever owned it was obviously a fan of yellow since the entire structure was painted the same shade as a sunflower. Only the roof, doors, and trim were different – a striking black.

"The garden isn't pretty right now. But once spring starts in full, you'll find the house gets a little more palatable."

I threw a smile at my boss. "You mean the greenery tones down the loudness of the yellow?"

He chuckled, "more like the riot of flowers distract the eye. Come on," he began walking up to the house. "Let's see how you like the place."

I'd applied as a carpenter with Thor's Shipbuilding back in Capricorn Cove. Gunnar, the owner, had put me through my paces and liked what he'd seen. He'd offered me a job, asking if I was willing to apprentice as a shipwright. Considering the woodshop where I'd worked for the last two years had gone bust thanks to shitty financial management, I was more than happy to go back to school and get some new skills. The best part was he was still paying me at full wage while I did the bridging course.

I'd left school early, apprenticing in order to set myself up for when the state would throw me out on my ear.

I was a foster kid, bouncing around homes until I'd wound up in Capricorn Cove with the McKenney's. They'd been a nice bunch. Generous with their time and love, sharing their little town with me and the other kids in the home. When I'd said I wanted to become a carpenter, they'd helped me out, ensuring I still got my high school diploma even while I got trade certified. When I'd aged out of the system, they'd helped me out, setting me up with a little apartment, making sure I had food, telling me that I'd always had a place at their table if I ever needed anything.

So, I'd stayed. Finding work with a local carpenter, designing custom pieces, working on houses, building cheap tables – in a small town like Capricorn Cove you had to be a jack of all trades. I'd enjoyed the work but loved the paycheck more. I'd been saving for a deposit on a home, still living in that first shitty apartment with its flaking walls and damp smell. It'd been cheap and a place to sleep. Nothing special but it worked for me.

Or at least it had until the workshop had

gone bust and I'd been forced to dip into my savings to continue covering rent.

When Thor's Shipbuilding had bought the marina, the town had been a flutter of excitement. I hadn't expected to land the job, but Gunnar had liked my work and I wasn't about to look a gift horse in the mouth. Most people took one look at me and made judgments about my ability to perform. I didn't blame them, but it still pissed me off.

Cape Hardgrave was the headquarters of the century old business. I'd done my research, looking into the Larsson's financial situation, what their employees said about them, client lists – the works. Thor's Shipbuilding were world-renowned, highly distinguished but small and boutique. The people who came to them paid top dollar for quality and name.

When Gunnar had said he wanted me to apprentice I'd agreed, willing to suck up the cost of living and moving for the apprenticeship period at the established headquarters. And when he'd said that it would be all-inclusive? Well, I'd practically thrown myself at the opportunity. It was like all my Christmases had come at once.

We walked up to the house; a ramp had been installed on one side of the stairs. I lifted an eyebrow in question.

"Our grandmother lived here before she moved in with my parents. She used a stick for a few years before graduating to a walker last year, though she mostly uses a wheelchair in public these days. The ramp was easier for her to navigate than the stairs."

I nodded, tucking that info away for later. While Gunnar sprang up the stairs, I navigated the ramp, following him up to the entry.

The entry consisted of a wide porch with sweetheart swings on either corner, little picture windows, and two black doors.

"You're in the first apartment." Gunnar turned the key in the lock, opening the door and leading me inside.

Beautiful wood floors, high ceilings, and white blank walls. The place felt empty but warm.

"It's your place," he said, leading me through the space. "Feel free to pop up art or pictures or move stuff around. We don't mind."

Those butterflies morphed into bats as I walked through the hall, grinning as Gunnar began the tour.

"Master bedroom with ensuite to your left. There's a small guest bedroom to your right. Linen closet in the hall," he opened the doors showing me a well-stocked closet. "If you need anything else linen-wise just buy it and hand the receipt to Ma. She'll reimburse you."

He gestured to a door on our right. "Main bathroom and another closet." He opened a door on the left. "Office space," Gunnar threw me a grin. "You'll need it. Erik is rigorous in his testing."

I chuckled, following him into a small living room, complete with comfortable furniture, a tiny dining room with round table, and a small but completely functional kitchen.

"You can open this up," Gunnar said, showing me how to open the large bifold doors onto the back deck. "Gets a great breeze year-round."

Now I could see why the house had been built backward – with the bedrooms on the road. The backyard opened onto a sloping yard with a magnificent view out to the ocean. The back porch was completely covered and I could see there were sliding screens to keep the bugs out. The yard itself was flourishing, beautiful greenery, and budding flowers ready to bloom in the coming weeks. A slight breeze tickled the hairs on my cheek; salt and pollen heavy in the air.

"This is beautiful," I told Gunnar, spreading my arms and sucking in a deep, satisfying breath. "'You're sure I'm living here rent-free?"

He chuckled, "oh, it's not rent-free. Erik's gonna work you hard. Don't have any doubts about that."

I laughed, following him back inside. "I look forward to it."

"Laundry's through here, all your utility access is in there too." Gunnar gestured at a door off the side of the kitchen. "Out the side of the house there's a single carport but it's got a small workshop at the rear. Feel free to use that however you want."

I nodded, taking in the gloriously retro kitchen.

"If you need anything else just call. Ma's put together a welcome pack, it should be around here somewhere. There are groceries in the fridge, and I have no doubt she'll be around later to visit." He knocked on the wall dividing my apartment from the one next door. "And my brother Rune should be done with work later. He's a little quiet, comes across as testy but he's a good kid."

"Kid?"

Gunnar laughed, "I mean, I guess not but—"

"Hello?" A voice called from the entry, interrupting Gunnar.

"Hey, come on down. We're in the kitchen."

What sounded like a stampede of people thundered down the hall. A woman, her dark brown hair streaked liberally with grey, a man who had to be Gunnar's father the resemblance was so strong, a woman who looked vaguely familiar held one baby, while a man who I assumed was Gunnar's brother Erik held another. They entered the kitchen in a jumble of limbs, smiles, and chatter.

"Gabby, meet the family. Well, some of them."

The older woman came in, dropping a basket on the kitchen counter and opening her arms. "Hi Gabby, I'm Jemma. Sorry, I'm a hugger!" she wrapped her arms around me, pulling me close.

I sent a deer-in-the-headlights look over her shoulder at the older man. He chuckled.

"Jemma, let the poor girl breathe."

She let me go, stepping back and slapping a hand on the older man's chest. "Ignore him, Gabby. Sune has no manners."

"My mother and father," Gunnar said, gesturing between the two. "And this is my brother, Erik, and his fiancé Laura, and their two boys, Ulf and Leif."

"Hi," I held out a hand and Erik took it, giving it a warm shake.

"Welcome to the Cape," he said, juggling the baby. "Hope you don't mind that we're intruding. Thought we'd pop out to help you move in."

"But first," Jemma pulled a sourdough loaf from the basket. "Lunch."

I was quietly but efficiently shuffled out of the kitchen and onto the back deck, a baby somehow ending up in my arms, while Erik, Sune, and Gunnar described the workshop to me.

"Obviously," Erik said, handing me a bottle of soda that had appeared as if by magic, "we're not expecting you until next week. But if you feel like coming and checking us out, let me know. I'll make sure I have some time to show you around."

"That'd be great," I said, dodging a flailing baby arm. "Gunnar said you were upgrading the workshop?"

Erik laughed. "Not the workshop itself, that'll have to wait till next winter when work slows a little. We're upgrading the office at the moment, adding a nursery." He nodded at his boys. "We're a family affair and these two have reminded me of that. We're adding the nursery so no one has to juggle family and work. They can do both happily."

"That's... wonderful," I said, lifting my drink in salute. "And super progressive."

"He just likes Ma's free babysitting," Gunnar said, knocking his shoulder into his brother. They both laughed and I smiled, watching them, already feeling at ease with my decision.

"Besides, with Laura's film schedule, I like to have the back-up."

I froze, drink halfway to my lips. "Film schedule?"

"I'm the Queen of Clean," Laura answered, stepping onto the deck, a platter laden with sandwiches in her hand. Jemma trailed, her hands holding two pitchers of drink.

"It's a reality TV show where I—"

"Clean people's houses. I've seen some of your social media clips." I leaned forward, glancing between her and Erik. "Did you meet on the show?"

They both chuckled, nodding.

Jemma sat, gesturing at me to start eating. "Please, we're not formal here."

Around food and drink, I learned more about the workshop, the business, and their family.

There were five children altogether,

Gunnar, Erik, Liv, Astrid, and Rune, but only Gunnar and Erik were part of Thor's Shipbuilding. Gunnar was engaged to Ella, who owned a bar back in Capricorn Cove. I'd met her a few times, a lovely bubbly woman, confident and warm. She was the reason Gunnar had bought the marina and moved to the Cove.

Erik and Laura had met on the set of her TV show when she'd been asked by Liv, who was a television producer, to help him out. Having just adopted twins, Erik had been overwhelmed by the responsibility and cleaning and needed some extra help.

I couldn't help but smile at the way they described their relationship, both of them

Gunnar had driven me up to the Cape but would be heading back to Capricorn Cove later tonight. The way his family teased him; I had the impression that he didn't like being away from his fiancé for long.

In addition to Gunnar, Erik, and Liv, there was Astrid and Rune. Astrid was away at college, completing her masters in architecture.

"And your other son?"

"Rune is—"

Leif let out a screech, his hands kicking angrily as he demanded to be put down. We laughed, his momma rolling her eyes.

"Let me just go swap out this kid's diaper."

"You want me to do it?" Erik asked, handing Ulf to his mom and moving to stand.

"No, Babe. I got it." She touched his shoulder on the way out, and he captured her hand, pressing a quick kiss to her palm.

I approved of both the intimate, tender gesture and his willingness to take on diaper duty. While I'd loved working with Gunnar, there hadn't been a guarantee that I would like his brother just as much. All that I was observing, from lunch to the way he interacted with his family, boded well.

We chatted some more, settling back as the midday sun warmed the deck. I could just imagine summer days spent here, listening to music, pottering around the garden, the breeze cooling my skin, sticky from the hot sun.

"-and you'll want to go to the Fire Ball which is coming up," Jemma said, interrupting my daydream.

"Fire Ball?"

"Mm, every year the town raises money for the fire department. They often fly out to help some of our neighbors during the season. We make sure our boys and girls have the right equipment for that."

"Sounds good," I said, refilling my glass

with the homemade lemonade. "Is there an auction? Or do we just donate or...?"

"There's always an auction. And the business purchases the table for our employees to attend," she fluffed her hair, sending Sune a grin. "It's an excuse for me to buy a new dress and look half-decent for a night."

Sune leaned over, pressing a kiss to his wife's lips. "You always look perfect."

She chuckled, waving him off, a slight blush heating her cheeks.

That kind of timeless love was so rare, my heart ached to experience something like that. Looking around at the table, seeing how loving they all were to each other, I ached to experience that kind of family.

One day.

"But aside from the auction and the Ball, there's all sorts of fundraisers in the lead-up. There's a pie drive, the local school holds a fair, and there's a fun run."

"Don't forget the readathon," Erik said, reaching across the table to snag the final chocolate chip cookie. "Rune, my youngest brother, runs it. You can sign up at the Literary Academy." He grinned, "it's a café-slash-bookstore. You'll want to go in the morning, Rune makes a mean cup of coffee."

"I'll check it out."

"Well, we should get you moved in." Erik pushed up from his chair, stretching.

"If you get the spare key, we can pop them down in Rune's place," Laura commented, digging through the diaper bag. "I think I brought a spare baby monitor and it's about time for their nap anyway."

"Don't worry," Erik waved a hand. "Rune has one."

They trooped next door while Sune, Gunnar, and Jemma headed outside with me.

The van was small, I'd only brought the bare essentials. When I'd decided to take up Gunnar's offer, I'd sold all my furniture, adding the proceeds to my dwindled savings. I'd done the figures - it would have cost me more to store my stuff than to sell it and buy new ones once I returned. The only things in that van were a custom cherry wood bed with beautiful matching side tables, a few boxes of clothes and some personal items. Two suitcases, a bike, and my spare prosthetics were in my car.

We moved it all inside in a surprisingly short amount of time, Laura diligently cleaning every item.

"You never know what it's picked up," she told me, brandishing a spray bottle and cloth. "Particularly in moving trucks."

Once my bed was rebuilt, and all the

clothes and whatnot popped away, the family called goodbyes, Erik reminding me to check out the Literary Academy. "Seriously, best coffee in America."

I laughed, waving them off.

In the silence of the house, I straightened a rug, dusted an imaginary piece of lint from the couch as I made my way through the house to the back deck once more.

Stepping into the sunshine, I raised my arms, throwing them out wide, closing my eyes and tilting my head to the sun. Gentle warmth heated my skin, the breeze teasing my hair. I could smell pollen and damp earth as it mixed with the salty bite that came from the ocean in the distance. I heard birds trilling, the soft rustle of leaves as the wind brushed through branches, and, if I concentrated very hard, the very dim crash of waves.

I opened my eyes, dropping my arms and resting them on my hips, grinning out at the view.

"Welcome home."

CHAPTER 2

Rune

I had to face it; this was going to be a shitty day.

In the grand scheme of things, I guess it wasn't that bad. But right now, I was damn grumpy.

The day had started off well enough. I'd woken, gone for a run, then tried to drive to work only to find I had a flat tire. Ordinarily, this wouldn't be a problem as I carried a spare. Only, I'd loaned the spare to my soon-to-be sister-in-law Laura for some segment she was doing for her socials. I didn't get it, nor did I care that much but it had been mildly annoying now that I needed it.

I'd sucked it up, pulled out my old bike, and

ridden into work. Where I'd found a late delivery from last night had been left on the back dock. The back dock which had been impacted by last night's rain. The books were ruined. And all of them had been part of an overdue delivery for eager readers desperate for an author's new release.

I'd quietly dealt with that issue, photographing the damage and writing a curt email to the dispatcher. We may have been a small store, but we punched above our weight in sales. I knew that the dispatcher had accidentally dropped that little tidbit when he'd last been out. There was no excuse for this nonsense.

By the time I'd opened the store, I'd been mildly inconvenienced. That had changed when the tourists arrived.

A large pack of young twenty-somethings with more money than sense, they'd tumbled through the doors of my store, laughing and disrupting my regulars for their morning coffees.

"Oh. My. Gawwwwwwd!" one of the girls squeaked, staring glassy-eyed at the book tunnel. "Quick, take my picture! This is so going on the 'gram."

I'd inherited the Literary Academy from my grandmother. The store had been failing before I'd taken over, added the café, bumped out the back, and created book sculptures to generate interest. It'd taken me about a month of eight-hour days to finish the giant book tunnel that separated the café from the bookstore. Booths lined the tunnel, positioned just so for people to have a coffee or wine, and read an hour away.

In addition to the tunnel, there were themed areas. Like in the kids' section, I'd created a pirate ship out of books that they could play on. In the romance section, there was a sculpture of lovers embracing. In gardening, there were flowers, and so on. I rotated the sculptures every month or so, refreshing some of the smaller ones to create new interest and generate new buzz online.

I'd realized early on that if I was to turn a profit, then I needed to reinvigorate my gran's idea of cool. As much as it pissed me off, making a photo-attractive business was generating a fairly decent return.

Even if people didn't buy a book, they at least bought from the café, so the trade was good. And foot traffic and pictures drove more foot traffic and pictures, which was good for the town as well.

Even if I hated it.

I cleared my throat, catching their attention

and tapped on the blackboard above my register.

Quiet, please. Don't disturb the other customers.

She flushed, her face taking on a mulish expression.

"And just who are you?" she demanded, hands moving to her hips.

I inwardly sighed. Yep, it was gonna be *that* kind of day.

I tapped the title embroidered on my chest, the one reading Head Librarian.

"The owner," I replied, gesturing at the filled tables around the joint. "You can take your pictures, just keep it down a little."

She sniffed, lifting her head and giving me a side-eye. "One star for service."

Her friends dragged her away, taking her into the bookstore while one of her friends stayed behind ordering them to-go coffees.

"Sorry about Shayna," the girl told me, leaning across the counter, positioning so her shirt gaped open at the neck. "She's still a little wasted from last night."

I shrugged, keeping my eyes on the frothing milk.

"So, you own this place?"

I nodded, quickly pouring the milk into the waiting coffee in the recyclable cups, adding a dash of froth, chocolate, or cinnamon as required.

"You doing anything later?"

I finished with the coffees, sliding them into a tray and across to her.

"Reading."

She laughed, rolling her eyes. "Oh, reading. Well, surely you could put that off and come out dancing with us later."

"No," I replied, moving back to the machine and beginning to make the next order, having just spotted Mrs. Howell hovering outside while her granddaughter diligently parked her tricycle.

The girl looked shocked for a moment then shrugged. "Whatever. Your loss. Weirdo."

She flounced off, coffees in hand, following her friends into the bookstore. I hoped Jill, who was on duty in there today, had clocked them early.

Mrs. Howell, her granddaughter holding the door open, entered, fluttering a hand to her face. "Oh my, it certainly smells good in here."

She made her way through the tables, calling greetings as Maisy danced about, handing out flowers she'd picked from her grandmother's garden.

The little girl had been living with Mrs. Howell since her mother had gone to jail.

Everyone in town knew, but we didn't talk about it. Just like we didn't talk about how Mr. Murphy and Mrs. Scree had been carrying on for years even though in public, they pretended to hate each other. And we definitely didn't talk about the fact Mr. Rodney liked more than one glass with his dinner and had to be regularly driven home at the close.

There were more secrets and unspoken bullshit in this town than I'd like, but it was home.

"What would you like today, Maisy?" Mrs. Howell asked, looking down at the girl.

Maisy rocked on her little heels, her lips pressed together as she considered the menu. Considering she didn't yet read, I had no idea what she thought to garner from her perusal.

I slid the Cappuccino, two shots with extra sugar, across the counter to Mrs. Howell, who took it gratefully.

"One muffin and a spwinkle cup," Maisy finally said, missing her r's.

"Coming right up," I replied, turning to the display cabinet and finding the muffin space empty. "Actually, give me a second, and I'll see if there're some fresh muffins in the kitchen."

I ducked out the back, finding another tray our chef had left cooling on the bench.

Returning, a woman stood at the counter. Long dark hair that complimented her high cheekbones and beautifully flawless complexion. Her lips were wide, painted a glorious red, and eased into a fucking gorgeous smile. Around her neck lay a turquoise-encrusted choker. She lifted one hand to toy with it absently as she perused the counter cabinets.

And just like that, the movement of her hand at her throat put me in mind of sex. Filthy, sweaty, dirty sex. Long nights spent in bed, my hand wrapped around her neck as I devoured her mouth, my cock buried between her thighs.

I felt like I'd been punched in the gut, such was my reaction to her.

Mine.

I had to attribute this reaction to the werewolf novel I'd been reading last night. There really wasn't any other explanation.

Fated mates aren't a thing, dickhead.

"Hey." The woman lifted her hand in greeting. Thick rings around her index finger and thumb glinted in the soft lines of the café. "You must be Rune."

"Uh, yeah."

She looked me up and down, interest warming her gaze even as she laughed. "I feel sorry for your momma. You guys are all massive. Viking stock, right?"

"Nordic heritage, yes." I popped the tray on the counter. "And you are?"

"Gabby, your new neighbour." She held out a hand, and I took it. Her grip was warm and firm, her fingernails painted black and white. Aviators were pushed up onto her head, tangled in her hair.

"You're the apprentice?"

She nodded, pumping my hand once, then dropping it as she glanced around the café. "Yeah, just here until October, maybe November depending on how my training goes." She threw me a smile. "Don't worry, I'll try to keep the noise to a dull roar."

I didn't know what to make of this woman. She wasn't at all what I was expecting when Erik had said they needed the other apartment. I guess I'd expected someone younger or less sure of herself. Not this bold woman who wore her body like she knew all the secrets of the world.

"Rune?" Mrs. Howell called. I looked her way, seeing her gesturing at Maisy. "Can you watch her for a moment, dear?"

I nodded, taking a muffin from the tray and placing it on the small plate I kept just for Maisy. Mrs. Howell headed for the restroom while Maisy made her way to the counter. I slid the muffin across to her, watching as she reached up, carefully sliding it off without dropping it.

"Take that to your gran's table, and I'll get your drink," I told her.

She nodded, balancing the plate, tongue poking out the side of her mouth as she tried not to drop the treat.

"What can I get you?" I asked Gabby, my hands moving automatically to pour milk and chocolate into a milkshake glass for Maisy.

"Can you do a caramel latte?"

I nodded.

"And I'll take a muffin to go." She frowned at the menu. "Gosh, everything looks good."

"Try the blueberry pancakes," I told her, knowing in my gut she'd like them.

She laughed, the sound delightfully rich and genuine. "I was just thinking about that. You totally read my mind. Let's do it."

"Excuse me." The little voice had us both glancing down as I finished making Maisy's drink.

"Yes, honey?" Gabby asked, a gentle smile on her face.

"What happened to your leg?"

I shifted, subtly glancing over the countertop to see Maisy touching Gabby's prosthetic leg. I tensed, waiting for Gabby to tell her to stop, but instead, she smiled.

"What do you think happened?"

Maisy bit her lip, screwing her face up as she squinted, thinking.

"A shark," she declared. "A weally, weally big one!"

"Nope," Gabby chuckled. "The only sharks I've met have been very friendly."

She leaned against the counter, one hand steadying her as she stuck her leg out. "Sometimes, babies are just born this way. That's what happened to me."

Her shorts cut off mid-thigh, revealing yards of leg. Her left ended just below the knee, a prosthetic making up the lower part of the limb. A bright pink compression sock covered her skin from just above her knee, disappearing into the prosthetic.

Maisy frowned, running her tiny hand up the carbon fibre limb.

"You didn't lose it?"

"No, honey. I never had it to begin with."

Maisy nodded. "It's pretty," she whispered, her fingers tracing the vines and flowers that decorated the leg.

"Do you like it more than my other leg?" Gabby asked, gesturing at the tattoo that decorated her right calf. The black tattoo was intricately detailed, a turtle swimming through the ocean, a map of the world on its back, only small parts marked by pops of color.

"I like this one better," Maisy declared, patting the prosthetic. "I like pink."

I finished making Gabby's drink as they chatted. Maisy's gran returned, calling her back to the table.

Gabby picked up her drink and packaged muffin, accepting their invitation to sit with them for breakfast.

"Food's up."

I picked up her pancakes, delivering them to the table.

"Oh Rune, you should invite Gabby to join the fundraiser," Mrs. Howell directed, laying a hand on my arm.

"Fundraiser?" Gabby asked cocking an eyebrow in my direction as she picked up her fork.

"Readathon," I told her gruffly, watching with unholy interest as she sliced a bite of the pancakes, lifting it to her mouth. "Raising money for the fire department."

"Ah, your parents mentioned something about that yesterday." She slid the bite between her lips, her eyes closing as she moaned, slowly chewing.

Fuck. I had to shift, adjusting my stance to

avoid anyone catching sight of my rapidly hardening cock. I hadn't been this horny since reading Kati Wilde's Hellfire Riders series. That whole week I'd been hard as a fucking rock.

Ask her out, doofus.

Don't fucking rush me.

I cleared my throat, frowning as I tried to work out how to ask her to dinner.

Been a while.

"This is so good. Thanks for the recommendation," Gabby forked another bite.

"Are you interested?" Mrs. Howell asked. "You just need to get some sponsors and for every book you read, they pay for it."

"I'm doing it!" Maisy piped up, playing with her paper straw. "Mr. Jennings said he'd give me a dollar a book!"

"Wow, that's awesome." Gabby raised a hand, slapping palms with the young girl. "But I'm not a reader. Maybe I can just sponsor our girl, Maisy here?"

My world screeched to a halt.

"Not a... you don't read?" I repeated.

"Uh-huh," she affirmed, licking her fork with a tongue that, only moments ago, I'd contemplated tasting.

I grunted, stepping back from the table. "Enjoy your breakfast."

I returned to the counter and the line of patiently waiting customers.

Sighing, I settled in, making coffee, serving food, and watching, with one disappointed eye, as Gabby quietly charmed Mrs. Howell and Maisy. She got up, placed a tip on the table, and called goodbye as she left, shooting me a smile and a wave.

I stared at the door for a long moment. Feeling eyes on me, I glanced over to find Mrs. Howell watching me, pity written across her face.

"I'm sorry, Rune." She shook her head. "I had high hopes for that one."

So did I.

CHAPTER 3

Gabby

I fed the wood through the saw, watching carefully to ensure the wood didn't buckle or slip. Once complete, I shut the saw off, lifting the cut and checking the line.

Perfect.

A flash of movement in the corner of my eye caught my attention. I looked over, pulling my earmuffs down, pushing my safety glasses up, and smiling at my new boss as he headed over.

"Hey, it's after five. The gang is clocking off, you wanna come for a drink?"

"Sure." I shifted the wood, laying it against my shoulder and following him as we walked back into the main construction space.

The new Capricorn Cove branch of Thor's Shipbuilding had nothing on the Cape workshop. This was a professional operation from top to bottom.

I could see why Gunnar had sent me here to learn – he wanted to replicate the processes and layout back in the Cove. But without seeing it and experiencing the flow and pulse, it would be almost impossible to understand his vision.

"How are you finding it?" Erik asked, tucking his hands into dusty jeans.

"Amazing," I told him honestly. "The guys are wonderful, and this workshop is just... next level, and the projects are really great."

He laughed, slapping me gently on the back. "We do alright. You'll let me know if you have any issues though?"

Apart from your little brother?

"Promise."

We chatted as we walked into the main workshop, pausing so I could lay the cut with the others I'd need next week. Thor's Shipbuilding complex was set up in a series of three warehouses, each interconnected. The shipyard consisted of the main warehouse where the ships were built and repaired. Within the main warehouse sat offices off to one side, including the lunchroom and the soon-to-be-completed nursery.

Upstairs was an apartment that had been used by Erik before he'd adopted his twin boys. Now it was empty, but I'd heard rumors they were only keeping it that way until the end of the school year when Astrid graduated.

The two outbuildings contained different workshops and storage. Giant in size, one had been divided into three, built to store wood and steel, with the relevant machines and tools ready to go. The last one was for critical work. A dust-free workshop set up for painting and fabrication. I'd watched in awe as one of Erik's men, Rafe, had demonstrated how to create a small fiberglass hull in less than an hour.

"You want a lift?" Erik asked when we made it to the locker room.

"Where are we going?"

"Literary Academy. They do beers and wine Friday and Saturday night. Oh, and for book club on Tuesdays – but it's mostly local women who attend. And Rune."

Damn.

I hesitated, my hand gripping the leather of my bag as I considered my options.

It was only my second week in the Cape, but I'd already fallen in love with the people, the location, and the work. I wanted to pack up, move here, and settle down.

Or at least, I wanted to except for one big, broad roadblock – Rune.

The man glowered at me, one big, gruff attractive lump of unfriendly mountain man. I'd visited the Literary Academy every morning this week, determined to get my caffeine fix and meet the locals.

The morning of my first full day in the Cape, I'd assumed Rune had maybe been interested. I'd liked the way he'd looked at me, approving and slightly heated. But day two had proven me wrong. He'd been curt, his jaw clenched and eyes dead as he'd served me. So, I hadn't gone back. Instead, I'd tried the other coffee places around town, quickly discovering that Erik hadn't lied – Rune's was the best in America. Or, in this case at least, the best in town.

So, putting on my big girl panties, I'd returned the following week, determined to ignore Rune's chilly reception. It wasn't easy, but his coffee made the bite a little easier to bear.

"Gabby?"

"Sorry," I pulled my bag free, settling it over my shoulder. "Yeah, I'd love a lift if you can."

"No problem, let's toss your bike in the back. Are you planning on riding home after drinks?"

I hesitated then nodded. "Can you give me a minute to swap my legs?"

"No problem," he grabbed his backpack, swinging it over his shoulder. "I've gotta grab something from the office. Meet you at the truck?"

I nodded.

He left and I pulled out my regular limb, sitting to swap it out.

I owned three different types of prosthetics, each serving a different purpose. My heavy-duty one was for work. It was specifically designed for standing for long periods, and for rough terrain. But it was graded as being suitable for heavy-duty work but didn't have the same flexibility and lightweight design that my every day held. The other two were every day, one really for general use, while the second was good for hiking and bike rides.

Most people only had one, maybe two. But I'd volunteered to be a part of a trial for a new lightweight, low-cost version. The carbon fibre with the pretty painting had been designed specifically for me in exchange for participating in the trial.

Once a year for the last three years, I took

myself off to Chesterfield Hospital to participate in testing and updates. It'd lasted me three years, though I'd had to swap out the socket last year due to some issues with pain. If all continued to go well, the company would be producing these in mass quantities within the next year or two. Affordable, durable, prosthetics. I couldn't wait.

I swapped out my leg, and decided to change my shirt, replacing the battered, filthy plaid with a nice plain black cotton. I washed my face, scrubbing dust from my skin, then ran a brush through my hair. It was only when I found myself looking for a tube of lipstick that I realized what I was doing.

"Stop it," I ordered, shaking a finger at myself in the mirror. "Rune doesn't even like you."

But it didn't stop me from wanting him too. God, he was just my type. Built like his Nordic ancestors, the man was massive. Bigger than both his brothers, broad and strikingly blonde. He wore his hair longish, with a slight bit of scruff dusting his jaw. I'd heard rumors that he used to have a man bun and full beard – but it'd scared Maisy so he'd cut them off.

A man cutting his hair for a four-year-old— be still my beating heart.

I locked up before walking out to meet Erik

at his truck, finding my bike already loaded. He was on the phone, sitting in the cab. I slid in, mouthing sorry as I closed the door. He brushed me off with a dismissive wave, starting the truck up and then putting his call on Bluetooth.

"Laura, you're on loudspeaker. Gabby's here with me."

"Hey, Gabby!"

"Hey," I replied, feeling a little awkward.

"I'm just trying to convince my bone-head fiancé to fly over to Chesterfield for the upcoming long weekend."

He sent me a *kill me now* look.

"Uh," I said, searching for a way to lighten the tension. "I didn't realize you were out of town."

"I'm not. I'm sitting at a table with the guys at the Literary Academy waiting for you guys to get here. But I want to book these tickets now."

I blinked, raising an eyebrow at Erik, who shrugged, shaking his head.

"Is there... a rush sale or something?"

"No, I just want it sorted."

"And I told you, Queenie," Erik replied, indicating to pull out of the shipyard then halting to wait for traffic. "If we're going to fly across the country to visit your family then we're going for longer than a weekend. I don't want your parents thinking I'm rushing off."

Behind us the automatic gates slowly closed, sealing the yard for the weekend.

"And *I* don't want to stay longer than we need to. The boys are finally in a good routine and—"

"Fine, book it. But add two days on." Erik told her, pulling out in the traffic. "I'll work it out with the team."

"Oh, they're here. Let me ask." There was an audible scramble on the other end of the phone.

Erik blew out a sigh, sending me an exasperated look. "Pray your future in-laws aren't crazy. Mine are cleaning freaks. I spilled a little airplane coffee on my pants the first time I met them, and seriously, Laura's dad made me take them off so he could deal with it. I met her grandmother in my boxers."

I sniggered, as Laura came back on the phone. "Ian says it's fine as long as you agree to let the boys off at lunch on the Wednesday before Gunnar's wedding so they can drive down early."

"Fine, fine." Erik rolled his eyes. "It's not like I have a business to run."

"See you guys soon!" Laura made a kissing sound then hung up.

Erik blew out a breath, shaking his head once again. "Are you flying or driving back to Capricorn Cove for Gunnar's wedding?"

I blinked. "Um, I didn't think I was invited."

Erik waved a dismissive hand. "All employees are invited." He turned down main, headed for the store. "We're planning on doing a road trip up, though God knows how that'll go with the twins. It's a six-hour drive. Do you know if they allow you to drug kids? Don't answer that."

I chuckled. "Are you sure? I mean, I've only been an employee for a few months and –"

Erik shrugged, turning into the parking lot and finding a space. "I'll check with Gunnar, but I'm pretty sure he's assumed you're coming."

I shifted, feeling awkward. "Is it a fancy wedding?"

Erik laughed, putting the truck in park and switching it off. "Not even close. It's gonna be a ceremony in their backyard, followed by a party. They've organized food trucks, rides, and games. The whole town is invited to see Ella shack up with my bro."

The clutch of anxiety eased. "Ah, so it's more like...." I tried to think. "Like a royal wedding. Where everyone celebrates."

Erik barked out a laugh, shaking a finger at me. "God, don't tell my brother that. He's got a big enough head as it is."

Chuckling, we both exited the truck, heading inside the building.

I'd only been inside the Literary Academy during the day. At night, it transformed. Soft lighting in the café, old-school reading lamps on tables, a live musician playing softly in the corner. Twinkle lights hung from rafters and guided people down the book tunnel, inviting them to get lost amongst the stacks.

"Wow," I muttered. "Wasn't expecting this."

Erik heard, shooting me a grin. "We used to go to a bar down from the shipyard. But Evan doesn't drink, so we started coming here so he could get a shot of coffee."

We found Laura and the other Thor's employees easily, they were arguing about what to buy Gunnar and Ella for their wedding.

At the table sat Ian, our foreman shipwright. He had a touch of Scottish brogue still in his tone, though he'd moved to America in his early years. He was big, broad, and incredibly red. From the top of his head to the tip of his beard, and all the way down to the hair on his toes, the man resembled nothing so much as a hairy red bigfoot. For all his size and hair, Ian was surprisingly refined, having surprised me more than once with his knowledge of wine, literature, and politics.

Beside him sat Jack, the youngest member of our group. He was studying marine architecture at college and had spent the last summer interning with this motley crew. If I'd been even two years younger, I'd have given him more than a passing glance. But the boy still had much to learn, and as I neared my late-twenties, I couldn't find it in me to want to teach him.

Gavin and Rodney were next. They were surprisingly thick as thieves for men who had virtually nothing in common. Where Gavin was all comedy and friendliness, Rodney was prickly as a porcupine. Gavin was a bit of a player, leading the women of the Cape on merry chases, while Rodney had settled down with his high school sweetheart, marrying her the week after graduation. They worked well together and had a wealth of experience that I was more than willing to bask in.

Our final two seats were taken up by Laura, Erik's fiancé, and Evan, who was sipping tea. He looked utterly at ease in the store, a stack of books sitting beside his teacup.

"You got any ideas?" Laura asked Erik, before pressing a welcoming kiss to his mouth.

"For?" He slid in beside her, wrapping an arm around her chair.

"Your brother's wedding gift."

"Nope. That's why I have you." He gave her a squeeze, shooting her a smile as he reached for her glass, taking a sip.

"Nah-uh," Ian said, shaking his head, his red shaggy mane flying. "She wants to get them a carpet shampooer."

I raised an eyebrow at Gavin in question. He rolled his eyes, tilting his head towards the bar. "You want a drink, Gabby?"

"I'll get it," I glanced at the table. "Anyone need a refill?"

Ian requested a chardonnay, but everyone else waved me off. As I walked away, Erik and Laura began to argue about why a carpet shampooer was a terrible wedding gift.

"Queenie, they have wood floors."

"But rugs! They'll need to wash the rugs."

I chuckled. Leaning against the bar, I picked up the drinks menu and quickly perused the options.

A glass of white wine and a mojito landed in front of me. I glanced up; eyebrow raised when I saw Rune watching me. Damn him, He looked good, his work shirt stretched tight over his chest, an apron tied at his waist. His face was blank, but his eyes held... something as he watched me.

Why do you have to be so attractive?

I wouldn't care half so much that he didn't like me if it weren't for the way he looked... and how he'd treated little Maisy that first day. I couldn't shake how gentle he'd been with her.

"For me?" I asked, nodding at the glasses.

"On the house," he said gruffly, moving about the bar to get another drink made.

"Uh, thanks."

Way to send confusing signals. Make up your mind, dude.

I reached for the mojito, took a sip, and found the drink slightly different to what I expected.

"Wow," I muttered, licking my lips. "Is that mango?"

He nodded, his hands moving in a flurry of motion as he tipped, shook, and stirred.

"Nice." I took another sip, considering him.

"Hey Rune," a young woman came up, leaning against the bar. I saw her interest in him, a small nugget of amusement threading through me when I realized he wasn't at all interested in her. Rune's body language shifted his back straightening, his body shifting slightly away from her.

"Florence," he greeted, finishing the pour,

then lifting delicate glasses filled with a cloudy liquid and placing them on a tray. "What can I get you?"

I sucked another sip, hanging around to watch.

"I'll have a cowboy cocksucker," she said, sending him a wink.

"We don't serve that."

I hid a smile, finding this immensely amusing. Not because I didn't support my fellow thirsty woman – sister, I was there for you. But because Rune looked so incredibly awkward as he tried to give her the brush off.

"Oh," Florence pouted, glancing at the menu and then holding it out to him, pressing her breasts to the bar, so they were more pronounced. "How about this one?"

Rune took the menu, closing it and placing it back in its holder. He got to work, making her a strawberry daiquiri in record time.

He placed it on the bar, taking her money. For a moment, Florence hovered as if waiting for him to take the initiative, but Rune had turned back to me, ignoring her.

"Maisy wants to know if you're still going to sponsor her."

Florence sighed heavily, looking disappointed but flounced off, sending a rueful smile and an eye-roll my way. I returned it, laughing as she mouthed *good luck* at me.

"Gabby?"

I turned back to Rune. "I promised her I would," I told him, finishing off my drink.

He took the glass then held up a bottle of rum in question.

"Yeah, another would be great."

As he made it, I considered him, the liquor likely giving me courage I wouldn't ordinarily have.

"Why do you hate me?"

His hands froze mid-motion. His body freezing as his head slowly turned towards me, surprise in every line of his face.

"Hate you?"

I nodded. "It's pretty obvious. You can't even look at me most days and I've only been here a few weeks." I shrugged, trying not to let him see how his reaction hurt. "I guess it'd just be nice to know what I did."

As Rune finished making my drink, a waiter returned to the bar with an empty tray. He picked up Ian's chardonnay handing it to him. "Could you take this to Ian, please?"

The guy nodded, whisking the drink away. I slid onto a bar stool, waiting for him to explain.

He grabbed a cloth, wiping down the bar as he pursed his lips, considering me.

"I don't hate you."

"No?" I raised an eyebrow, circling my paper straw in the glass, swirling the mango syrup. "Sure about that?"

He blew out a breath. "Sorry. I just find it hard to meet new people."

I lifted an eyebrow. "Really? You're gonna Mr. Darcy me?"

He blinked. "You've read Pride and Prejudice?"

"Geez, don't sound so surprised. Just because I don't love to read doesn't mean I'm illiterate."

Not to mention Colin Firth makes me thirsty as fuck.

"And," I continued, more than a little annoyed at him. "if it did, that's a massive strike against you for being a prejudiced dick."

If the fact he was running the damp cloth over the exact same spot repeatedly was any indication, it looked like I'd surprised Rune.

"Touché. I guess I get a little touchy when someone states they hate something that I adore." He frowned. "So why won't you join the readathon?"

I rolled my eyes. "I don't know Rune,

maybe because I don't enjoy reading? Or maybe because I don't want to."

He tilted his head to one side. "What was the last book you read?"

I absently sipped the mojito, trying to remember. I had to stop a shiver when Rune's gaze dropped to my lips, his eyes darkening a fraction.

I shrugged. "I don't know. Probably an instruction guide your brother loaned me."

He shook his head. "Not non-fiction, fiction. What was the last book?"

"Can't remember."

Rune's face flushed, his lips thinning into one disapproving line. "So, you haven't given books a chance."

I rolled my eyes. "God, I don't know. What's your beef with this?"

"Do the readathon. Read, let's say, twenty books of my choosing, and I'll sponsor you a thousand dollars."

My eyebrows lifted. "Excuse me?"

"Twenty books, a thousand dollars." He crossed his arms, glowering at me.

"Ten."

"Fifteen."

"Done!" I slapped a palm on the bar and then held my hand out to shake. "You can't back outta this one, bucko."

His hand encompassed mine, warm and solid and ridiculously large. His eyes glinted as he shook my hand, giving it a tiny squeeze. Something sparked between us at the contact, a shiver of awareness racing down my spine.

"You can pick up your first books tomorrow." He held my hand for a beat too long before turning away to serve a new customer. I picked up my glass, taking a long, badly needed drink.

Oh, joy.

CHAPTER 4

Rune

I woke to music. For the third Saturday in a row, I woke to music streaming through the wall beside my head.

Gabby, I'd learned, didn't know the meaning of quiet. She woke to music and played it through her morning routine. She chattered to the birds and flowers outside as she ate breakfast, she sang in the shower and yelled at the TV.

And the thin walls of our duplex hid nothing from my ears.

For years I'd lived beside my grandmother, assisting her and ensuring she had what she needed to get by. When that situation became untenable due to needing around-the-clock assistance, she'd moved in with my parents. That had been two years ago, and I'd grown used to the quiet.

Gabby was an unpleasant, unwelcome shock to the system.

You sure about that bud? asked my erection.

I groaned loudly, reached for the spare pillow on my bed, and pulled it over my ears, attempting to block the noise.

These days, I had weekends and Friday nights off. When I'd taken over the store, I'd worked around the clock to ensure it was a success. Now that we were financially viable, I'd eased up, hiring more staff to take on the work and allowing me to concentrate on the business side.

But in the last few weeks, a gastro-bug had hit the local elementary school, and most of my day staff were single parents so I'd been forced to fill in. It wouldn't usually be an issue, but it just so happened to coincide with the lead-up to finals, which meant my college students were on restricted hours. I'd pulled more hours this month than I had in a while.

Ordinarily, I didn't mind. But after three weeks in a row with only one day off, I was pretty wrecked. I had the afternoon shift today which meant a slight sleep in and I was going to relish it.

The music switched from pop to rock and then to an acoustic mix.

My eyes drifted close, my breathing evening out as I started to fall back to sleep.

A crash shook the bed, jolting me awake. A startled shriek and more crashing followed.

Gabby!

I scrambled out of bed, dashing to our shared rear deck and around to Gabby's back entry. The door was open, and inside I could see a trail of destruction.

"Gabby!" I bellowed, running inside, head swinging wildly about as I tried to track the scene.

Fuck. Fuck! Where is she? Fuck!

"Help! I'm in the bathroom!"

Her voice was muffled, and I had an immediate vision of her hiding from an attacker.

I bolted through the house, down the hall, past the empty main bathroom, and into her room, stumbling to a halt at the door.

Her room was trashed. The trail of destruction began on her back deck, continued through the living room, down the hall, and had its grand finale in her bedroom.

Lamps and picture frames lay broken on the floor. A basket full of laundry had been tipped over, the clothing now strewn about the room. A prosthetic leg lay between the bed and the ensuite door, looking as if it had been discarded in a hurry.

The music abruptly cut off as I stared at the giant pelican sitting in the middle of Gabby's bed.

"Ferdinand!" I barked, placing hands on my hips. "What the fuck man?"

The ensuite door opened a fraction, Gabby's poking her head out.

"Wait, you know this beast?" she squeaked, her eyes wide, hair a rioting mess.

"Unfortunately."

Ferdinand raised up, flapping his wings wide, making a low, hoarse, almost barking sound in greeting.

Gabby opened the door a little wider, hopping to lean against the jamb as she stared at the monster on her bed.

"My grandmother was a wildlife rescuer. Ferdinand is one of the nestlings she saved." I sighed, taking in the mess. "He normally stays in the garden but might have freaked out when he saw you instead of Nan."

Gabby pressed her lips together as

Ferdinand began to groom himself, looking for all the world like he was in for the long haul.

"And your grandmother just let him walk through the house?"

"Sure."

She shook her head. "Can you pass me my crutch? It's in the closet."

I glanced her way, taking in her tiny sleep shorts and her thin black cotton t-shirt. She was braless, her hair wild, missing a leg as she leaned against the doorway, her expression begrudgingly amused.

Gorgeous.

My erection, or what had remained of it after the Ferdinand intrusion, roared back to life, my cock thickening and lengthening.

Fuck.

I wore only boxer briefs and a thin sleep shirt, the material hiding precisely nothing from her.

Fuckity fuck a fucking fuck.

I twisted abruptly, heading to the closet, opening the door, and blinking in surprise.

"Oh, yeah. Watch out for the body parts."

Parts for her prosthetic sat on shelves in the closet. Different types of feet and sockets. Finding the crutch, I pulled it free, carrying it over.

"Thanks." She tucked it under her arm, hopping to readjust her weight. Now comfortable, she finally looked me over, her lips quirking a little as they landed on my raging erection.

"Ignore it," I said gruffly. "I do."

She tilted her head, her eyelids lower, a warm flush coming to her cheeks. "I didn't realize pelicans were your thing."

I barked out a laugh. "Yeah, that and being woken by screams from my neighbor."

She chuckled, then nodded at the pelican currently making a nest on her bed. "So, how do I get rid of him."

I sighed, running a hand over my cheek. "Don't laugh."

She blinked. "Excuse me?"

I mentally girded my loins, knowing this was about to hit a whole new level of strange.

"Just... don't laugh." I turned to the pelican, giving him a stare. "Hey, Ferdinand."

He looked up from his preening, giving me a dark-eyed stare. "Do you have time to sing a goodbye song before you go?"

Behind me, I heard a strangled laugh and sighed again.

Ferdinand flapped his wings, gargling at me.

"Goodbye, goodbye, Ferdy, goodbye.

'Cause now it's time to go, but hey, I say, well that's okay, cause we'll see you very soon, I know," I crooned, making a gesture at him to get off the bed.

With a happy flap of his wings, he hopped off the bed and began to waddle out to the hall. I continued to serenade him with a bastardized version of the goodbye song from the children's TV show *Bear in the Big Blue House* as he finally made it outside, Gabby following us.

"The moon, the pelican, and the big yellow house will be waiting for you to come and play. Come and play. To come and play." I gently slid the screen door shut behind him, calling. "Goodbye now, Ferdy."

With a final bark, he flapped his wings then took off, heading back to the water.

Behind me, Gabby snorted, the strangled laughter spilling free. "Oh my god," she leaned on her crutch, clutching it as she bent over slightly, her laughter bellowing out. "Oh my god!"

I blew out a breath, mentally counting to ten.

"You know," I said mildly, gesturing at the mess. "I was gonna help you tidy up, but now I'm thinking you don't deserve it."

She finally calmed, wiping away tears of

laughter. "That was, by far, the weirdest and most enjoyable morning I've had in years."

I cocked an eyebrow and she chuckled.

"I stand by my statement." She tilted her head. "Is your nan still alive? Cause she sounds like a real character."

"Yeah." My heart punched a little. "She's still alive and kicking. But she had a stroke and finds it harder to get around now, not that she'd let us know it. Still just as crazy."

"You'll have to tell her Ferdy came by." She started giggling again. "And that you rescued me from the bathroom with a song."

I sighed. "You're gonna tell my brother about this, aren't you?"

"Oh, yeah."

I crossed my arms in front of my chest, giving her a glare. "Well, just for that, I'm gonna make you add the Bible to your reading list."

She laughed, straightening and repositioning the crutch, shifting to move into the kitchen. "I'm sure my sinner butt could probably use some words of wisdom."

"More like forgiveness," I muttered.

"Coffee?" she asked from the kitchen.

I shook my head. "Nah, thanks, though. But I've got to get to work." I looked around at the chaos. "Actually, I'll get dressed, then come and help you clean. Can't leave it like this."

"You sure?" She lifted the handle of her coffee pot. "Won't take me two minutes to pop a pot on."

My lips quirked. "I'm sorry to say but I don't do instant anymore. My tastes are a tad more refined these days."

She rolled her eyes, replacing the pot. "Sorry I don't have an espresso machine for you, Mr. Bourgeois."

"Oh, a fancy burn from the woman who doesn't read," I teased back.

"Hey, just because I don't read doesn't mean I'm not intellectual."

I held my hands out. "Point well made."

I dropped them, still trying to ignore the throbbing ache in my cock. "If you want a good coffee, I'll bring one over. Unlike you, I do have an espresso machine."

She blinked. "Holy shit. You been holding out on me, Rune?"

My name on her lips did something to me. Something I liked a whole hell of a lot.

Down boy.

I shrugged. "Give me a few to shower and dress, and I'll bring a cup over."

"You do the coffee; I'll bring breakfast."

"Done."

We split, both of us dressing, me having the world's quickest (and coldest) shower. Her music started back up as I finished dressing, tying off my shoelace. I made us coffee and then carried over the cups. As I entered the house, the music switched, and the intro song for *Bear in the Big Blue House* began playing.

"I guess you don't want this coffee." I pivoted on my heel as Gabby, sputtering with laughter, called out a protest.

"Don't! I do! I really need some of that sweet, sweet elixir. I'm sorry... well, not totally. But it was worth it."

I turned back, finding her holding one plate in each hand.

"I made French toast..." she said, holding one plate out to me and then the other as if she were trying to entice me over. "Come on, you know you want some."

Yeah, I do.

I came in, placed the mugs on her counter and took the offered plate. We ate side-by-side at her breakfast bar, Gabby chatting, me listening and, surprisingly, enjoying her chatter.

After, she popped the dishes in her dishwasher while I took stock of the mess. It wasn't as bad as it had initially appeared. A few broken picture frames, some knocked-over ornaments, an upended side table. The main damage was in the bedroom.

"I'll get the dustpan and broom," she said, heading for the laundry.

Together we worked quietly and efficiently, setting the place to rights once more.

In the bedroom, we cleaned the floor and then considered the mess of feathers on her duvet, including a small tear.

"Washing machine, then I'll see if I can save it." Gabby decided.

We removed the feathers, stripped the bed, and quickly placed all the linen in her washing machine.

While I waited for her to finish straightening the bedroom, I walked around her living room, taking in the photos and numerous photo albums stacked on the mostly empty bookshelf.

"Nice family," I commented when she came back in.

Gabby paused, a stack of papers Ferdinand had displaced in her hand.

"Thanks, but they're not actually my family." She looked back down at her papers, flicking through them again, sorting them into some semblance of order. "I just collect them."

I frowned. "Collect?"

She lifted one shoulder in a shrug, "You

know, some people collect paintings, I collect photographs."

I glanced at the wall again, taking in the posed family snaps, the black and white images from bygone eras, and the slightly fuzzy candids.

"Where do you get them?"

"Garage sales, antique stores, estate sales. Sometimes I pick them up at Goodwill," she waved a hand at the albums stacked on the bookshelf. "Family pictures are rarely sad. More often, they show joy. But these were discarded. And it feels wrong that something that was created in good times is discarded because of misfortune."

"Whatcha mean?"

She pulled a paper from the stack, setting the others aside as she turned to me. "People don't give away happiness. The reason these photos are now with me isn't because they intentionally decided to discard them. It's because something happened. Either people passed, or they fell on hard times or any number of things. So, I collect them. Good times deserve to be celebrated."

I blinked slowly, staring anew at this woman. A woman I realized I'd fundamentally miscategorized from the moment we'd met.

This woman is deeply layered. I thought she

was a standalone novel but she's a series. A universe. A creation that would keep you hooked for decades to come.

"What's on your list for today?" she asked as if she hadn't just rocked my world.

To kiss you.

I cleared my throat, fighting the sudden ache I had inside me to hold her close, to love her, to build a life with her.

Pull yourself together, dude.

"Work." I gave myself a mental shake. "I should probably be heading there now."

She nodded, biting her lip and tipping her head slightly to the side. "I should come in to get my list, yeah?"

"List?"

She grinned. "Of books?"

A sudden surge of lust hit my gut. An image of Gabby reading a book in bed beside me materialised. She'd be dressed in that thin cotton t-shirt and tiny sleep pants. We'd be reading the same book, a romance I'd picked out for us. We'd read the same scene at the same time, both of us getting hotter as the leads stroked and caressed, speaking filthy, dirty things to each other.

I shifted, attempting to hide the fact my cock was pressing against my zipper. My dick heavy and hard. It seemed to be a new normal around Gabby.

"Right," my voice sounded off. Deep and low, a little gravelly, hoarse. "Come in later, and I'll work it out."

"Just not the Bible, okay?" She laughed, the sound did nothing to help ease my need.

"We'll see."

Father forgive me because I'm about to sin.

CHAPTER 5

Gabby

As I rode my bike into town, I found myself distracted by the image of Rune standing in my room. He'd looked like a conquering Viking – if Vikings wore boxer briefs.

Despite being a woman of the world, a woman used to looking after herself, I couldn't deny that it had been nice to know I had backup. Granted, the backup had only been required to serenade a pelican from my room, but the memory of big, wild-eyed Rune bursting into my house to slay the dreaded pelican invader had lit a warm little pool of pleasure in my belly.

Not to mention that erection. Phew! Girl, go get on THAT!

Ah yes, the erection in the room. That tent in his briefs had proved one thing – the man was big *everywhere*.

My body gave a delightful shiver remembering how he'd looked at me. It was as if I were a dollop of cream, he couldn't help but want to taste.

And that in and of itself was a marked moment. It wasn't that men didn't find me attractive; I knew they did. I'd dated on and off over the years so I'd had a lot of experience with men who were happy to date me as long as I didn't show them the real side of my life. The side where I sometimes needed to use a crutch and where I needed a stool in the shower.

It didn't bother me, but people with no experience of disability often struggled. They didn't have the words or know how to ask the questions. They made assumptions or talked down to me as if my leg missing meant I was somehow less capable of making decisions.

I'd assumed Rune was like that. That he'd taken one look at my prosthetic the first day and decided I wasn't worth the trouble. But today had me reassessing that assumption.

The man had looked at me like he wanted to lay me on the bed and eat me from top to toe.

He'd not handled me with overt care, instead just getting me what I needed, ensuring I was okay before getting on with it.

He was fucking with my head and emotions, and I didn't know if I liked it.

But I definitely don't hate it.

I parked my bike out the front of the Literary Academy. The café was crazy busy, people spilling onto the chairs and tables outside. The smell of fresh coffee, warm baked goods, and a citrus tang sat heavy in the air, inviting people in.

In the few weeks I'd lived in the Cape, I'd yet to visit the bookstore. The café, sure, no problem. The books? Not really my jam.

Also, if I was honest with myself, I felt like a bit of an interloper. Rune hadn't exactly been friendly, and I hadn't exactly made an effort.

Gird thy loins, Gabby. We're going in.

I pushed through the old wood doors and entered... wonderland. Inside, the store was cool and smelt of old books. The kind of smell that reminded me of libraries, old scotch, and a crackling fire, though only the Lord knew why.

The store was larger than it first appeared. The Literary Academy occupied old warehouses. The brick walls were left bare, same with the timber beams that made up the soaring ceilings. The space would have felt large and somewhat sterile if not for the dividers.

Each section was marked by things hanging from the roof and towering sculptures made from books or paper. There were lights strung here and there, creating little places to draw the eye. As I walked further into the store, I found myself getting lost in a maze of shelving, stumbling across a lover's nook or a surprising art piece, a reading area, or a pirate ship made from books.

Acoustic music gently played through carefully hidden speakers, and it felt like such a world away from the bright bustle of the café next door. I suddenly understood why Rune had created the book tunnel. Without it connecting the two, gently guiding a person from the bright into the calm, it would be a shock, all impact lost.

"Excuse me?" I asked a woman who was seated at a small table in what looked like a replica of an old study. The small nook was complete with a beautiful desk, leather seats, a globe, and an old desk lamp.

"Yes?" she asked, raising an eyebrow.

"Can you tell me how to get to the counter? I'm a bit turned around."

She chuckled. "You've not been here before?"

I shook my head.

She nodded at the shelves. "If you keep the shelves with a white line on their bottom on your right, you'll find the counter."

"Thank you."

I followed the line, backtracking my steps and winding around until I found the carefully positioned counter. It didn't sit at the front of the store as I'd anticipated. Rather, it was tucked beside the tunnel, an old-school cash register decorating the front of a desk. Books were piled on either side and behind the counter was a giant bookshelf that stretched up the whole back of the warehouse wall. All the books were black, except those in various russet shades, which together made up the words, *The Literary Academy*.

I hovered, waiting my turn as Rune stood behind the counter, serving an old lady.

"I distinctly remember it having a blue cover," the woman said, peering at the book in her hands.

"You said it's a romance and has a character named Greer." He nodded at the book. "That's it."

She shook her head. "No, I don't think so."

He pressed his lips together and then nodded. "How about you try this one, Maeve, and if it's not the book you want, then I'll try and find it for the next time you're in?"

She frowned. "But I don't want to read this book. I want the book with the blue cover."

"And the person named Greer?" he asked.

She nodded.

He held up a hand for a moment as if thinking. "Okay, give me a moment."

Rune headed out from behind the counter, another staff member immediately taking his place to serve the next customer. A few moments went by before he returned, carting a book with a blue cover.

"I think I might have found it. It's by Sierra Simone. But Maeve, *American Queen* is racy. As in, it's got a little threesome action in it. And it's part of a trilogy. You okay with that?"

Can I get Rune to add that to my list?

She eagerly reached for the book. "That's the one I was thinking of."

"You want the other books in the series?"

She nodded, already opening the novel to the first page.

He left and returned a moment later carrying two more, ringing up the sale. "You want me to add these to your list?"

"Please."

She paid, then headed through the round door, which looked slightly like a door from that movie about the Hobbits, then into the tunnel headed for the café.

Rune turned, catching sight of me lurking like a stalker. His lips quirked into a smile.

"Feeling nervous?"

"Puh-lease," I told him with a wave of my hand. "I'm gonna own this challenge."

He grinned, leaning on the old desk. "Okay, tell me three things you like."

"What kind of things?"

"I don't know, movies, music, you tell me."

I thought about it for a moment. "I like period dramas, Sons of Anarchy and Star Wars."

He nodded, that same look he'd given Maeve crossing his face. "Be right back. Ash, can you get Gabby set up on the X-list?"

"Sure thing, boss." The girl had been scanning books into their system. She had bright red hair, a lovely smile, and wore a Literary Academy shirt that read, Geeky book girl.

"I like your hair."

"Thanks! My old job would never have allowed it. It's why I love working here." She pulled a tablet out from under the desk, giving it a quick wipe with an antibacterial cloth before handing it over. "If you could just enter your details, we'll get you all signed up for the readathon."

I read the terms and conditions, checking over the information. I entered my details hit submit then handed it back. While I'd been doing that, she'd been printing out some documents. She handed them over.

"The top sheet is your sponsorship sign-up. You'll get this all in an email as well so you can post to social media and get more sign-ups. People can pay just a lump sum or can pay by the book. You list the books you read below, and then one of our members will send you three questions about it. If you get them right then we know you've read it."

I raised my eyebrow. "Wait, this involves a quiz? I didn't realize I was back in high school."

She laughed. "Two years ago, we had a member who registered for the readathon. She said she'd read two hundred books in the two months. It only took Rune three minutes to discover she hadn't read even half. So now, to make sure sponsors aren't getting ripped off, we check."

I nodded, looking back down at the sheet. "Why's it called an X-list?"

Ash pointed at a large blackboard on the far side of the door. "Normally we have our recommendations up there. Over the summer, we track people's reading tally. The more X's you get, the more money we have coming in. Hence, the X-list."

I nodded, looking at the many marks on the board. "Looks like a decent fundraising effort."

"Oh yeah, it's second only to the street fair. Are you doing the parade this year? Erik always puts on a great float."

"Sorry?"

How does she know where I work?

She laughed, her hair shimmering in the soft light. "This town is pretty tight-knit, gossip spreads like wildfire. And Laura attends Tuesday night book club when she's in town." She disappeared behind the big old desk and then stood up, handing me a flyer. "You should totally come. It's mostly just women gossiping and drinking wine, but we do share book recommendations as well."

I looked at the flashy flyer.

"The Greedy Readers Book Club?" I asked with a laugh.

"Yeah, because we're insatiable."

I grinned, liking her even more. "Tuesdays, you say?"

"Uh-huh. Wine, we normally split antipasto platters, and always gossip."

"Count me in." I tucked the flyer in my back pocket.

"Great!" Ash practically vibrated with excitement. "So, are you gonna be on the float?"

I blinked at the sudden change of topic. "Huh?"

"The Thor's Shipbuilding float. For the parade for the fair. Last year they did an under-the-ocean theme and all the guys dressed up as mermaids. The year before that they did Gilligan's Island. Erik was Ginger."

I laughed, trying to picture it in my head. "Well, no one's mentioned anything yet."

Ash flapped her hand. "Probably 'cause it's not till the end of August. We've still got time." She grinned. "But you should casually mention to Erik that we've already designed our theme for this year and it will be *epic*."

"Don't tell her all our secrets," Rune said, returning to the counter, a pile of books under one arm.

"I'm just saying. We're winning this year; I can feel it." She looked at me. "It's a bone of contention each year as to who places higher – Thor's Shipbuilding or the Literary Academy. The brothers go all out."

"And who won last year?"

"Oh." She cackled while Rune rolled his eyes. "Neither of them ever wins. That always goes to the art school. But we're hopeful about this year." She held up crossed fingers.

A customer waved from between two stacks, calling for assistance.

"I got it," Ash said, turning to help. "See you Tuesday, Gabby."

"See you," I called as she disappeared into the stacks. "She's nice."

Rune nodded then dropped his gaze to the books he'd placed on the counter. "You ready?"

"As I'll ever be." I sighed, making a face.

He grinned, then picked up the first book on the pile.

"Julia Quinn, The Viscount Who Loved Me." He held the book up. "Second in series but you don't need to read the first, and I think you'll like the humor in this one more." He popped it down, lifting a bright yellow book.

"Educating Caroline, Patricia Cabot. Again, historical, again great humor." He placed that down, reaching for the third book. "Nina Levine's Storm MC. It's about a motorcycle club. Intrigue, suspense, love. You'll enjoy it." He held up another, and I burst out laughing at the cover.

"Is that a blue guy... with *horns*?"

He grinned. "Let me introduce Ruby Dixon's Ice Planet Barbarians. You'll read this one and beg me for the others. They were our top-selling series last year." He placed it on the pile. Then hesitated, his hand hovering. There were three books left.

"You can choose your fifth one – more motorcycle, another historical, or something completely different."

I cocked my eyebrow. "What do you mean by completely different?"

He shook his head. "You just have to decide."

I looked at the covers then reached out, touching the different one. "Okay, I'll give this a go."

He moved to place the book on the pile but I took it, reading aloud.

"Kiss of Steel by Bec McMaster." I flipped it over, scanning the blurb. "Honoria Todd has no choice. Only in the dreaded Whitechapel district can she escape the long reach of the Duke of Vickers. But seeking refuge there will put her straight into the hands of Blade, legendary master of the rookeries. No one would dare cross him, but what price would he demand to keep her safe?"

I looked up, shooting Rune a grin. "Have you given me only romance novels, Mr. Larsson?"

He shrugged. "Romance novels are the best novels."

I laughed. "Is it a historical?"

"Kind of. It's steampunk."

I wracked my brain, trying to remember where I'd heard that term before. "Oh, like Howl's Moving Castle?"

He nodded, looking impressed. "Actually, yeah. Kind of like that."

"Cool." I returned the book to the pile. "So, these five are my starter kit?"

"Mmhmm." He rung them up for me, then asked if I wanted a bag.

"No, it's fine." I pulled off my backpack, handing it over. "I came prepared."

He loaded the books and I paid, wondering if now would be a good time to invite Rune to lunch.

"So," I said, leaning against the counter. "I don't know about you but—"

"Fancy seeing you here!" Erik's big voice boomed in the quiet, interrupting me.

I turned, seeing him and Laura, a bouncing baby strapped to each of their fronts, enter via the Hobbit door. Behind them trailed Jemma and Sune, Sune pushing an older woman in a wheelchair.

"Gabby," Erik greeted. "Have you met Grandmother Larsson?"

I shook my head, moving to greet the older woman. "Mrs. Larsson, it's lovely to meet you. I'm staying in your beautiful home."

The older woman smiled but it was a bit wonky, one side not quite lifting. Rune had mentioned a stroke, and I now understood why she needed to live with her son.

"Call me Nan. Rune said Ferdy paid you a visit this morning." Her words were slightly slurred and a little slow but I understood her perfectly.

"Ah yes, or the winged assassin, as I've started calling him."

She laughed delightedly. "I like that."

"Would you like to join us for lunch?" Laura asked, one hand on baby Leif's back as he snuggled into her. "We're here to drag Rune out for a bite as well."

Rune sighed, gesturing at the shop. "Told you, I gotta work."

"Oh hush," Jemma said with a dismissive flick of her head. "This is your mother's orders. You don't rest enough. We'll only be an hour."

Before my eyes, Rune changed. He shifted from the loose, quiet but amusing man I'd been getting to know, to the near-silent wall of muscle I'd first met.

I frowned, glancing from him to his family.

Rune crossed his arms over his chest. "And what happened last time?"

The family laughed.

"Lunch went for two hours, it's not that big a deal," Sune said, shrugging.

A muscle jumped in Rune's jaw, his face flushing. I saw it. I saw the change, and yet it was as if no one else did. Not his nan, not his parents or brother. Not even Laura.

Only me.

"Come on. Do as your mother says," Sune ordered, wheeling Nan around. "We'll find a table. Don't be long, your grandmother is hungry."

I hung back, waiting until his family had left before turning back to Rune. His eyes were on the door, that muscle in his jaw still jumping.

I looked at him, wondering how far to push this.

"Are you okay?"

He blinked as if only just realising I were still there. "What?"

"Are you okay?" I repeated, gesturing at the door where his family had disappeared. "They completely ran roughshod over you."

He blew out a breath, watching me wearily. "And you think I should go to lunch?"

"No, I think you're busy and have a store to run." I gestured at the customers hanging around, the boxes of new books he was obviously processing behind the counter, and the sandwich sitting half-eaten behind the counter.

"I'm gonna assume that's yours?"

He shrugged. "Doesn't matter. Give me a second to call, Ash."

I leaned across the counter, halting him with a hand to his arm. "Rune, you don't have to give in. If you're too busy, tell me. I'll make excuses then keep them so busy and entertained and just utterly dazzled by my sheer brilliance that they won't even notice you're not there."

His lips didn't move, his expression didn't change. "They won't accept that."

"And you seem to care too much about what they expect versus what you want or, in this case, need to do." I squeezed his arm. "Trust me, Rune. I got this."

He searched my face for a moment, looking for... something. Reassurance maybe?

"Okay," he finally said. "Thanks."

"No problem." I waved a hand, pretending to flick hairs out of my face. "Just call me Lady 'cause your family is gonna go Gaga for me."

Only the very corners of his mouth lifted. "Good luck."

I turned, carrying my backpack with my hand-picked books, making a mental note to interrogate him more about this later.

He may be large and growly, but Rune obviously hated disappointing his family.

And God, why on earth do I find that attractive?

As promised, within a few minutes of sitting down with Rune's family, I had them sufficiently distracted with stories of Capricorn Cove while waiting for our food to arrive.

"Now, Gabby." Nan held her knife and fork at a jaunty angle, giving me the kind of smile I imagined a shark wore right before it ate the sweet little fish it was hunting. "Tell me, are you interested in my grandson?"

I blinked, shooting a look at Erik. "Umm, no? I mean, he's a nice guy but it kind of looks like he has his own family thing going on and I'm really not the kind of girl to get involved in a polygamous relationship – not that there's anything wrong with that but it's not for me."

A beat of silence followed my comment everyone at the table stared at me.

Nan tutted under her breath. "Not *that* grandson. The single one."

Her comment broke the tension, sending the rest of the table into hysterics.

She shifted her line of questioning, beginning to gather a background profile on me. I'd watched enough cop shows to know that she had to have been a detective in a previous life.

"And what do your family do?" she asked after I'd told her about how my previous jobs.

"Ah, actually, I don't have family."

The delicate skin on her forehead wrinkled. "You're an orphan?"

I shrugged. "Maybe. Who knows? I've been a ward of the state since I was a few months old."

"But you said your last foster home were pretty good. Do you stay in touch with them?" Erik asked, juggling a fussing Leif.

I shrugged, trying to ignore how these questions prodded the familiar ache in my middle. "They were my last home, and partially the reason I settled in the Cove. But I came to them at a pretty bad time. The McKenney's were great, don't get me wrong. But Mrs. McKenney was diagnosed with breast cancer a few months after I moved in. They had bigger problems than me."

Nan opened her mouth but Leif, god bless his little soul, let out a high-pitched screech, big fat tears rolling down his red little cheeks.

"He's been very fussy today," Laura told the table as Erik excused himself to take Leif outside. "I think he might be teething."

"A little whisky to the gum," Sure said tapping his lips. "Works every time."

"Don't tell them that!" Jemma slapped his arm, laughing when he turned to her and pressed an exuberant kiss to her cheek.

I looked around the table, experiencing a familiar sense of melancholy. Was it possible to miss what you'd never had? Not love, though I'd never had what Sune and Jemma did.

No, it was family connections that made my soul ache. The familiarity that came with years and experience, inside jokes and shared memories. The beautiful family before me had that.

It's not for you, remember?

I'd tried. Many, many times I'd worked hard to entrench myself into a family. I'd changed, and twisted, becoming whoever the family needed me to be. But eventually, after years of rejections and sudden movements, I'd resigned myself to the fact there was something wrong with me.

I just wasn't family material.

It didn't stop me from wanting it though. Desperately.

CHAPTER 6

Rune

I'd built a reading nook in the garden a few years back. A pergola with passionfruit vines under which there was a long semi-circular bench seat, wide enough to stretch out and lay on.

Sometimes, like this afternoon, I carried out a low table, complete with a pitcher of lemonade and an antipasto platter. Stretched out, enjoying the afternoon sun while I read, was how I unwound from a hectic week at work.

It was here that Gabby found me. Soft piano music playing from a Bluetooth speaker, the afternoon sun warm on my face, and a great book in my hands.

"Hey," she called softly, pulling me gently from the story.

"Hey." I marked my place with a finger. "What's up?"

She held up the yellow book in her hand. "I was just looking for a place to get started."

I grinned, scooting down one side of the long seat to make room. "Sit down, stretch out."

She did, settling in, our feet only inches away from each other.

"Can I have a glass?" She nodded at the lemonade.

"Sure." I pulled a glass free from the stack. Neighbors or family were always stopping by, so I'd learned to bring extra.

We sipped and nibbled our way through the afternoon, reading in quiet companionship. Me, a crime thriller, Gabby the historical romance.

"This is good," she murmured at one point, turning the page. "Like, really good. Do you think they've made a movie?"

I made a sound of displeasure. "Even if they had, the movie is rarely as good as the book."

"Purist." She chuckled, glancing up. "I can't actually remember the last time I read a book and enjoyed it."

"What was the last book you read? And don't say a manual this time."

Gabby's lips lifted in a smile as she tilted her head back, considering my question. "Maybe... maybe something at school? I just remember being fed up with the crap they were assigning us."

I grunted, shaking my head. "Schools need to update their material. The thing that pisses me off the most is you have a whole generation of kids you could be engaging by giving them relevant material. Really good material. Instead, you shove stuff they can't relate to down their throat. Like ninety percent of it is written by CIS white males. Kids need something to inspire them. Something that they feel. Not some adult asking them to describe in a thousand words why a dead guy described the curtains as blue when we all know he probably didn't even pay attention to what color he assigned."

Gabby stared at me for a moment, then burst out laughing, her body shaking with her hilarity.

"What? Am I wrong?"

She shook her head, still laughing.

"Exactly." I pretended to begin reading again, opening my book with a flourish.

"You should've been an English teacher."

I shrugged. "Thought about it, but then Nan got sick and needed help at the store and... well... it just fit."

We were quiet for a while, and my eyes strayed to my book, beginning to scoot down the lines of the page, slowly being sucked back in.

"Rune?"

"Mm?" I blinked, looking up.

Gabby hesitated. "How come your family treats you like that? Like what you're doing isn't a real job or something."

I shrugged, grabbing my bookmark and putting the book aside. "It's not that they don't think it's a real job it's more they just forget I'm an adult."

"Huh?"

I laughed, the sound slightly frustrated. "I'm the baby of the family. Eight years separate me from Gunnar, and there's only eleven or so months between him and Erik. They grew up together. Then there's Liv and Astrid, then me. I was more like a doll for the girls to play with than a little brother to tag along. I've grown up, my family just hasn't realized it yet."

She eyed me, her gaze drifting up my legs, across my chest, and finally up to my face. I tried not to react, liking the way she looked at me far too much.

"It's hard to believe when they see you that they don't immediately realize you're fully grown."

My lips quirked. "Have you seen the size of my family?"

She chuckled. "True. Your poor mother."

We returned to reading. In companionable silence, we continued until the night encroached, and our stomachs began to rumble.

We split a pizza, staying outside until the mosquitos drove us back to the covered porch.

I sipped my beer, Gabby sitting in one of the chairs, drinking tea. As the hour grew late, Gabby began to squirm. Not a lot, just enough that I noticed her breath catching and becoming more rapid.

I tried to ignore her, tried to silence the little voice in my head that was wondering which part of the book she was reading. I tried and failed to ignore the question that kept playing over and over in my mind.

Was she getting turned on?

Gabby let out a little moan. Low, barely audible, her breath catching. The sound snapped the little control I had left. My cock jumped, thickening embarrassingly fast in response. My body heated, my focus immediately narrowing in on her till I couldn't take it anymore.

"Gonna head to bed," I muttered, pushing to my feet and walking to the door. "Night."

"Night," she called, her gaze burning into my back as I left.

I headed straight for my bedroom, unzipping my pants, not even bothering to shove my jeans all the way down my legs.

I fisted my cock, roughly jerking my length, my spare hand braced against the wall as I imagine Gabby alone, reading that fucking novel.

As I stroked, I imagined her in bed, the book in one hand, her other drifting across her breasts, teasing lightly. Down her body it would glide as she devoured the naughty words, imagining it was me doing those things to her.

I groaned, fisting harder, fancying I could hear her through the wall.

"Rune."

I froze, my body solid, straining to hear.

"Oh, Rune...."

Through the wall, through that piss-poor excuse of a wall, I could *hear* her. Her little mews and whimpers, then the electric pulsing buzz of what could only be a vibrator.

My heart thumped against my ribs, my

body shuddering as I listened to Gabby pleasure herself.

"Fuck," she whimpered. "Oh, God."

My hand began to move of its own volition, stroking my cock, my eyes drifting close.

"Please," Gabby begged. "Oh, please."

"Louder," the word exploded from me, guttural and desperate. "Louder, Gabby. I wanna hear it."

Through the wall, I heard the buzz change, as if she had dropped it. There was a pause, brief but devastating.

Fuck.

I lifted, getting ready to move, to go apologize for intruding. But the buzz changed again, Gabby moaning in response.

"Rune... keep going."

CHAPTER 7

Gabby

I can't believe I'm doing this. What the hell? I pressed the vibrator closer, hitting the button to change the pulse setting, teasing myself, drawing this out.

Rune's listening.

The book had gotten me hot. The slow build-up, the way the hero was gentle but fierce with the heroine. I'd been sucked into the story, hook, line, and sinker.

But this? Right now?

Amazing.

"Let me hear you, Gabby. I wanna hear your hot little moans."

Rune's voice sounded above my head,

filtering through the thin wall. I shuddered, a groan slipping free as I circled my clit.

"Louder," Rune barked, his voice rough and demanding.

Desire spiked through me, lighting my nerve endings on fire. I moaned, writhing on the bed, my body a wanton, desperate creature.

"Rune," my voice sounded unfamiliar. Breathy, low, an aching need audible.

"You want me to describe what I'd do to you?"

I licked my lips, my free hand pushing up my shirt, reaching under the cup of my bra, fingers finding my nipple.

"Yes," I whispered, then cleared my throat, raising my voice. "Yes, please."

"If I was in there, Gabby, I'd be stripping you naked while I kissed every inch I revealed."

I shuddered, my body tingling at the images his words painted.

"I'd pull those goddamned sleep shorts down your legs, then lick my way up your thighs. I'd taste you, determined to memorize you. Would you be spicy, Gabby? Or sweet? Would you taste of salt and sea? I wanna know, babe. I wanna taste those thighs and then see you wearing those goddamned shorts and remember my lips brushing your skin."

Oh lord.

This man was killing me.

"Turn the fucking vibrator off," he ordered hoarsely.

I hit the button, discarding it easily.

"Fingers," he told me, his voice rough. "Use your fingers."

My hand drifted between my legs, hovering above my curls.

"How?" I asked, feeling surprisingly bold.

"Part your lips. Pretend I'm there, pretend I can see everything. Show off for me."

I did as directed, spreading myself with one hand, imagining Rune at the end of my bed, his gaze hard and needy as he stared at me, watching me circle my clit, my body flushed under his gaze.

"Are you wet, Gabby? Tell me."

"So wet," I breathed, circling my clit with firm presses, my fingers sliding easily through my slick arousal. "God this feels good, but..."

My desire overrode my sense of self-preservation.

"But?" he prompted.

"Wish it was you."

I heard his groan full of need and desire, heavy and guttural. I shuddered and increased my pace, driving myself higher.

"Rune!"

"Come, Gabby. Come now. Show me, let me hear."

I arched pretending he was before me, his gaze hot and focused on my fingers, on the way I rubbed myself, on my pretty pink pussy. I spread my legs wider, my body on full display as I finally shattered, my body clenching as I came in a glorious, sweaty, wet mess.

Through the wall, I heard Rune join me, his groaning gasp a maddening tease that flared my arousal once again.

"Rune," I whispered, stretching a hand out to the wall, pressing my palm flat to it. "Come over."

"Fuck yes."

I heard him move, shuffling about then freezing as the sound of his mobile's ringtone pierced through the quiet.

"Fuck!"

I heard him answer, then silence as he listened.

"I'll be right there."

More shuffling as I pushed up, quickly setting my clothes to right then heading out to the front porch.

"Rune?"

He came to the door, a backpack on his shoulder, his face grim. "Leif's in the hospital, they think it's just a fever and gastro, but Erik and Laura are freaking out and want me to take Ulf while they stay with Leif. Ma and Dad aren't answering the phone – they're probably out on the boat with Nan, they do that when they can't sleep thanks to the heat. So, I'm the only backup they got at the moment."

I nodded, reaching out. "You need a hand?"

He paused, eyebrows shooting up. "You wanna come and babysit?"

I bit my lip but nodded. "If you need me."

He seemed torn, wanting me to come but not wanting to burden me.

I smiled. "I'm offering, Rune."

"If you want..."

"Let me grab some stuff and lock up."

CHAPTER 8

Gabby

They may still treat Rune like a kid, but they sure as hell trusted him to be an adult when it mattered. We arrived at the small hospital, finding Laura and Erik a frantic mess.

"Here." Erik handed Ulf to Rune, his hair standing on end, his eyes bloodshot and rimmed with dark circles. "If he starts vomiting, diarrhea or any signs of fever—"

"We'll bring him here," Rune said, accepting the diaper bag from Laura.

"We wouldn't ask this but if it's contagious...." Laura reached out, placing a hand on Ulf's back.

"He'll be fine."

Erik caught Laura around the waist, pulling her tight. "If the fever breaks and they can get more liquids into Leif, we should be discharged tomorrow."

"Then you guys can come pick Ulf up tomorrow night. You'll need some sleep." Rune told them, shifting his nephew into the crook of one arm.

I didn't know much about babies, but I'd been quickly learning since moving to the Cape. Being around Erik meant being around his family. When they said Thor's Shipbuilding was a family business – they meant it.

"Thank you," Laura whispered, tears glistening on her lashes. "I don't know what we'd do without you."

Rune shrugged, looking uncomfortable. "Go look after Leif. I—we've got this."

Erik and Laura looked my way for the first time since we'd entered the hospital waiting room.

"Thank you," Erik said, giving me a small smile. "You didn't have to come out."

I waved him off. "Go look after your baby."

Laura and Erik turned as one, hurrying back to their son.

"You ready?" Rune asked.

I looked up, about to answer then realized

he was speaking to Ulf. Ulf grinned up at his uncle, his chubby little arms flailing.

"Right, let's go."

I reached for the diaper bag but Rune shook his head.

"Nah, I got it."

I'd been surprised to learn that he had two baby seats in the back of his car. When I'd asked why he'd shrugged.

"Just being a good uncle."

My heart had skipped, a warm shimmer gliding down my spine to pool in my belly at his words.

He strapped Ulf in with surprising efficiency then we were headed back to our place.

His place, dummy. Not ours.

This night wasn't exactly going how I had planned. Or not planned, in this case. I hadn't expected to get myself off with Rune listening through the wall, giving directions. I also hadn't expected to be looking after a baby less than an hour after one of the hottest experiences of my life.

Shouldn't I be embarrassed about this?

I found I didn't have either the modesty or shame to care that much. I'd loved it, and, I had to admit, I wanted more.

Rune turned on the radio, then switched to a playlist, calming classical music pumping out.

I lifted an eyebrow in his direction.

"It's a baby classical music list. The music is shown to help them feel calmer and happier. I figure, with his brother missing, our little guy needs all the help he can get."

I grinned but turned away before Rune could see exactly how much I liked his efforts.

Be still my ovaries.

This man was dangerous. He looked like a Viking god, was a doting uncle, read romance (hello great sex life), and was a hard worker. There had to be a downside.

"Are you messy?" I asked, genuinely wondering where the downside was.

"Huh?"

"Messy. Laura met Erik while teaching him how to clean. Are you also messy?"

He scoffed, shaking his head as Ulf gurgled from the backseat. "Hell no. My brother is the anomaly."

Hmm.

"Can you cook?"

He nodded, shooting me a questioning glance.

"I'm just trying to figure out your flaws. So far I can't find any beyond the whole reading prejudice."

The grin that stretched his lips was devastating. My heart skipped, butterflies scattering.

"I'm sure there are many more, but I'm happy to keep you in the dark."

He pulled into the driveway, parking just by the porch.

We climbed out, Ulf sleepily mumbling a protest as Rune lifted him out of the baby seat.

"Come on, little dude. Bedtime."

I followed, carrying Rune's backpack and the diaper bag. Rune pressed through the door to his apartment, and I followed, expecting the mirror image of mine. Instead, I stopped dead, looking around in wonder.

The place was one giant art piece.

The entry hall was a massive mural that stretched up and across the ceiling, incorporating the basketweave lights.

"Is this the inside of a boat?" I whispered, reaching out a hand to touch the wall. The art was so life-like it was jarring to feel plaster instead of the polished wood of a ship.

"A longboat," Rune said, opening the door to his spare room. "Let me put him down."

I followed, my gaze dancing from one unique item to another, shocked by the detail and effort.

The spare room was no different. Rune had

turned it into a nursery. Hand-carved cribs sat end to end against one wall. Toys were spread out across the floor, while a heavy shag rug in green covered most of the floorboards. There was a changing table and a rocking chair in one corner. The walls were covered in floating shelves that were filled with books, all for children.

The walls were again murals, this time a kid's version of a Viking scene, complete with a dragon hiding treasure, mermaids, wolves, and even a crow peeking out from behind a bookshelf. In addition to the Vikings on the longboat – all of which bore a striking resemblance to his family –Valkyries were riding in on flying horses.

"No wings?" I asked, touching a horse as Rune placed Ulf in his crib.

"In Norse mythology, Valkyries rode horses who could fly through air or ocean – but there are no mentions of wings. That appears to be from Greek mythology and doesn't fit the scene."

I threw him a grin, watching as he switched on a small night light, the soft glow pulsing gently through the room.

Ulf was out, his tiny body rising and falling with each breath.

Rune turned on a baby monitor, then

picked up the other device, carrying it with him as he gestured for me to follow.

I dropped the bags in the corner of the room, then, with a last look at Ulf, tip-toed out.

The rest of Rune's house was just as stunning. There were burnished bronze art pieces, sculptures made from books or wood, little drawings on walls – some in frames, some hidden amongst the furniture, like a tiny image of Ferdinand that sat above an electrical socket, as if resting on the edge.

And everywhere I looked, there were books. I couldn't help but grin.

"This is incredible," I whispered, once again reaching out a hand to touch a wooden piece. It was a coffee table, but the tabletop had been carved into a map of the world, the grooves inlaid with a bronze resin. It glinted in the dull light, shimmering just a little.

"Is this by a local artist?" I asked, running a hand over the beautiful wood. I wanted to create something like this.

"Uh, kind of. You wanna drink?"

I pulled back my hand, turning to see Rune in the kitchen.

"Sure."

He put the kettle on, waiting for it to boil as he busied himself, pulling out mugs and herbal tea.

I reached for the canister, reading it aloud, "peppermint?"

"Nan got me hooked. It was all she'd drink before bed."

I chuckled, replacing the canister and watching as he went through the age-old ritual of measuring out the tea leaves. It felt comfortable, familiar.

Like home.

I squashed that thought. I was only here for six months. After that, I'd be headed back to the Cove. Rune's place was here, with his family. I could see that. They needed him. And he was a part of the community, his business essential.

And you're not.

I knew it. I was disposable. Always had been, always would be. Years of foster homes and failed promises of adoptions had proved that.

It also doesn't pay to get involved with your bosses' brother.

I took the offered drink, inhaling the sweet scent before taking a sip, mentally resigning myself to this conversation, mentally building my walls.

"Rune, this can't go further."

His face wiped clean. "Excuse me?"

"This." I gestured between us. "Your

brothers are my bosses. And I'm leaving. I have to go back to the Cove. It doesn't make sense to take this further."

A muscle in his jaw jumped, a mulish expression settling.

"So, you'd throw away whatever possibility we have, whatever potential may be between us, because of distance?"

"It's not just distance. There's my job too. I want this career. This opportunity is important to me. It's going to help me secure my future."

"And you think if we didn't work, I'd jeopardize your career?"

I shrugged. "Wouldn't be the first time a woman has had her career derailed by a spurned man."

"I'm not like that."

"I know." I sighed, staring at my tea. "But I know where I stand. Family comes first. They'd pick up on the issues between us and want to show loyalty. They'd never fire me – they're too nice for that. But they might make it so I decide to leave."

"They wouldn't."

"Maybe not intentionally, but it would be the result all the same."

"Gabby—"

Ulf's cry split through the house.

"I'll get him," I said, jumping down from the seat at the counter and heading for the hall.

"Gabby, wait."

I picked up my pace, desperate to put distance between us. Tears burned my eyes, blurring my vision.

It was the reason I didn't see the toy on the floor. The bloody toy.

"Fuck!"

I tripped, crashing to the floor.

"Gabby!"

Ulf cried harder at the sound, but Rune came to me, his hands gentle as he searched my body for injury.

"Where are you hurt?"

"My pride?" I muttered, groaning as I rolled over.

Rune's hand paused on my leg. "Damn, it was the toy, wasn't it?"

I nodded, pushing myself to a seat and examining my leg. Everything looked fine, except for the bruise forming on my knee.

"Damn," I brushed myself off, shifting to begin the slow push to stand. "Give me a second."

"Here." Rune held his hands out, wiggling his fingers invitingly. "I'll pull you up."

I took it, letting him haul me to my feet, sucking in a breath and leaning into his chest as

I realized my prosthetic had moved, pain ratcheting up my thigh.

"Can you help me to the chair?" I asked, leaning heavily against him.

I expected him to help me hop over, instead, Rune lifted me, easily carrying me the few steps across the room. He gently set me down, making sure I was okay before stepping back.

"Go get Ulf," I said with a wave. "I just need to adjust it."

The fall must have slipped one of my liners, not a lot, but enough to shift it so when I put weight down, it was painful.

I pulled my leg off and began the long process of removing liners and socks, peeling them down to the end of my leg.

"Can I be rude and ask some questions?" Rune asked as he bounced Ulf, soothing the baby.

I looked up, shooting him a grin. "You wanna know what I call her?"

He blinked. "What?"

"My leg. Some people call them a stump which is offensive and makes me feel like I'm gonna sprout leaves and roots. I just call her Peggy."

His lips quirked as I patted my leg, his eyebrows raising in a question.

"You know, like a peg leg." I made a pirate arr noise.

He grinned but shook his head. "I was actually gonna ask if you get hot in all those layers."

"God, yes," I kicked my leg at him, enjoying the air on my overheated skin. "It's not so bad during the day, but I have to wear a shrinker sock to bed. Not because I'm an amputee but because I get inflammation. It sucks, some people don't have to, but I'm not one of them."

"What's it do?"

I patted my leg. "Helps to fit my limb into the prosthetic. Without it, it's painful."

"Huh, I guess I just assumed it'd be fitted for you."

"Oh, it is," I said, starting to pull on the liner. "But even a small amount of water weight or swelling can change the fit. So that's why you have these." I held up a sock. "You pad out or reduce depending on what's happening."

"And you do that every morning?"

"Yeah." I rolled on the silicon, checking the fit before feeding the pin into the shaft and locking it into place.

"I didn't realize it was like a pin-lock system."

"Not all of them are. I have three, and each is slightly different."

"Hmm."

Rune turned back to the crib, Ulf now sleeping again. As soon as he shifted the baby, Ulf woke, his hands and feet kicking out in protest.

Done with my leg, I stood, making my way over and placing a soothing hand on the baby's back.

"You just miss your brother, don't you little one?" I cooed, subconsciously swaying in time to Rune's movement.

He held Ulf up, giving him a narrowed-eyed glare. "You're not sleeping in my bed tonight, bucko. You know that. I already said no to you and your brother last time."

Ulf kicked his legs happily, a small drool bubble forming at the side of his mouth.

Oh, he was so gonna get his way. Lucky kid.

I hid my smile, stepping back as Rune resumed his sway.

We watched each other, our eyes holding.

"You know, I don't date," Rune said finally, his voice low as Ulf snuggled back into his uncle's chest.

"Oh, I realized that when you rejected poor Florence."

He blushed. "She's not interested in me anymore than she is in reading the works of Jane Austen."

I chuckled. "So, she wasn't hitting on you?"

"Oh, she was." He hesitated. "But she's more interested in winning the bragging rights."

I cocked an eyebrow. "For a date with you?"

He shook his head. "For sleeping with me."

"What?"

Rune blew out a breath, "I'm a virgin, Gabby."

CHAPTER 9

Rune

No one ever believed me when I said I was a virgin. I was a guy, for one. And yeah, it might be cocky but I knew I was attractive – my brothers were, so it only stood to reason I was aesthetically pleasing as well.

It wasn't that I'd made a conscious choice to remain sexually abstinent. And God knew I wasn't a saint – I watched porn, read erotica, and fisted my cock regularly.

But I just hadn't met a woman where the timing – and relationship – worked out. In high school, I'd only had to bring my girlfriends home for them to fall in love with Gunnar or

Erik. In college, there'd been one or two that might have come close – if not for Nan.

God, how pathetic did it sound to blame my grandmother for my lack of game?

I read. I read a lot. I knew I'd take over the bookstore when I returned to the Cape, so I decided to get a head start on knowing my product. Nan helped with that. She'd send me a new book box every month, packed full of novels for me to devour.

Though she'd include her favorites – the romance ones in particular. Which, never bothered me. I liked a good romance. But kids were idiots and the jock fuckwit of a roommate I'd been saddled with had seen them and spread the rumor that I was gay – as if it were a curse or some other ignorant shit.

I hadn't cared, except that women hadn't looked at me after that. When I'd finally come home, Nan had suffered her first bad spell, and I'd moved into the house, converting it into a duplex (a man needed his own space). Then it'd been either work or caring for her. There hadn't been an in-between.

Well, not until last year. These past twelve months I'd finally been able to let up and breathe. As hard as it was to say, Nan moving in with my parents was a blessing, and, while difficult, the best thing for both of us. I loved her, but I no longer needed to be her carer. She got more companionship and support from my retired parents than from me.

So yeah, I was still a virgin. And the shocked look on Gabby's face was nothing new. Any time someone found out they did that same stare, the one that said *what's wrong with you?*

Answer, not a goddamned thing.

"I'm... surprised," Gabby said, tucking a stray strand of her dark hair behind her ear. "I wouldn't have said you were a virgin after... earlier."

I chuckled. Ulf turned his head burrowing deeper into my chest, a little drool wetting my shirt. "I'm a virgin, not an idiot."

She laughed, her teeth flashing in the dim room. "Touché."

We both quietened, a comfortable silence falling over the room.

"You know, sex would change this," Gabby whispered.

I'm counting on it.

I nodded, peeking down at Ulf.

"It's not that I don't want you, Rune. It's that...."

I waited, wondering if she'd admit it.

You're scared.

She shook her head. "If you're good here, I should go to bed."

I nodded, disappointed she was taking the easy way out. "Yeah, okay. You should get some sleep."

She came to us, pressing a little kiss to Ulf's cheek. "Call me if you need anything?"

I nodded; my throat full. She gave me a smile, running her finger gently across Ulf's cheek one last time before leaving.

I listened, hearing her walk out the front and head next door.

"Fuck," I whispered, shaking my head. "She's gonna be harder to win over than I thought."

Ulf gurgled sleepily and I grinned. "Don't worry, buddy. I'm not deterred that easily."

My phone beeped. I pulled it out, the family chat icon blinking.

ERIK

Leif's fever broke. They're keeping him overnight just to be sure and top up his fluids. Looking good otherwise.

LIV

THANK GOD!

GUNNAR

Call if you need us, Ella and I are on standby.

ASTRID

Keep us updated and give little
Leif a kiss from me.

I hit reply, awkwardly snapping a picture of Ulf sleeping in my arms.

RUNE

[Photo] As you can see, Ulf is
very worried. Good to hear
he's on the mend. No rush to
come pick up, we're good.

ERIK

Thanks bro, appreciate it.

LAURA

Tell Gabby thanks too.

"Ah, damn."

LIV

Gabby?

ASTRID

?!? GABBY?? WHO IS
GABBY???

ELLA

Wait, OUR Gabby?

GUNNAR

Fuck. You break her heart and
we're keeping her over you.

ERIK

^^What he said. That girl deserves better than this family.

LAURA

Hey! What does that mean!?

ELLA

Excuse me!?

LIV

Oh, you're in for it now. Rune – should I add her to group chat? Someone text me her number.

Suddenly, I found I didn't mind their ribbing quite so much.

CHAPTER 10

Gabby

You're a wimp.

It took me a full three days to get up the courage to see Rune again. Now it was Tuesday evening and I was standing outside The Literary Academy psyching myself up to go in.

"Hey! Gabby! Hey! You came!"

I twisted to see Ash bouncing along the sidewalk towards me.

"Yeah, I finished all my books."

"Ooh! Yay!" She reached for the door, holding it open so I could enter. "You'll still have to pass the test."

She chattered on about the latest book while leading me through the maze to the seating area. About ten women were seated on various couches and love seats, glasses of wine in hand as Rune walked around, topping up their glasses.

Our eyes met, his immediately dropping to my legs, narrowing in on the bruise on my knee.

"You okay?" he asked, coming to stand next to me.

I nodded, remembering that night. While I'd had only minor bruising on Peggy, my naked knee had smacked the floor pretty hard, leaving a dark blue bruise.

"Hey everyone, this is Gabby," Ash gestured at me, bouncing over to sit beside an older woman. I spotted Laura and made a beeline for the seat beside her. She smiled a greeting, handing me a glass.

"How's Leif?" I asked, gratefully accepting the wine.

"Back to normal. Though God knows Erik and I have more grey in our hair than we did last week."

I chuckled, taking a sip of the rich red wine. "I'm glad."

She considered me over the rim of her glass. "Thanks for helping with Ulf."

I shrugged. "It was all Rune, to be honest. I just tagged along to the hospital to make sure he didn't crash in his haste to get there."

She let that one slip as an older woman called the meeting to order. Turned out, Ash hadn't been kidding – this was a wild, *wild* group.

It started off with a male appreciation circle, where we all had to name our favorite male of the week based on their 'talents' if you get what I mean. We then segued to books we'd read and loved, which somehow ended up in a discussion about the best sex toys on the market and the oldest member of the group, Beryl, discussing a thing called *'the dictator'*.

I'm telling you – W.I.L.D.

"This is honestly, the craziest night I've had in a while," I whispered to Laura. Only, my voice came out louder than anticipated, causing the other drunk women to laugh uproariously.

"It's the best," Laura agreed, slightly slurring her words.

The night wound down, partners appeared to pick up their women. Erik waved as he escorted Laura out. I laughed as she kept groping his ass, sending me exaggerated winks over his shoulder.

"You want a lift home?" Rune asked as he cleared the last of the books from the coffee table we'd occupied.

I blinked, realizing I was the last person in the store.

"Oh." I rubbed a hand over my face. "No, I should be fine to ride."

I pushed to my feet and immediately reached out, searching for something to steady myself as the world shifted.

"Oops! Maybe not." I giggled.

Rune chuckled, coming over to help me. "Let's get you in the car and I'll lock up."

"Wait!" I pulled back a little, pointing at the X-board. "You haven't asked me the questions. Go!"

Rune's lips quirked. "Which books did you finish."

"All of them."

His eyebrows rose in surprise. "Really?"

"Uh-huh."

"Huh, not bad for a non-reader."

"Psh." I blew a raspberry his way. "I'd say I'm now a reader, thank you very much."

"We'll see." He moved to the board, picking up a piece of chalk and holding it at the ready beside my name. "Okay, first question – Educating Caroline. What was Caroline surprised Brandon read?"

I pursed my lips, trying to remember. "The dictionary!"

He grinned, marking a cross.

"Not three questions?" I asked.

"Not tonight. We need to get you home."

I let it slide.

"Okay, next book. The Viscount Who Loved Me, the siblings played a game, what was it and what was Kate's equipment called?"

I laughed, delighted that he referenced my favorite part of the entire book. "Pall Mall and the mallet of death, of course."

He made another notch on the board. "In Bec McMaster's Kiss of Steel, what does Honoria offer Blade?"

"Speech and etiquette lessons instead of becoming his mistress." As Rune added another cross, the wine loosened my tongue. "But really he only accepted so he could seduce her. Like I wish you would."

Rune froze but I didn't pay him any mind. "Or maybe you'll declare I'm your mate and just wake me with your mouth on my pussy, like those blue alien dudes. Or maybe like when Kick pushed Evie up against the wall and fingered her." I brushed hair back from my face. "I'd like that. God, so much." My body practically vibrated with need.

"What about you leaving?" Rune asked, staring at me intently.

I tried to clear the fog in my head, instead finding the fog was clearing the lies I'd been telling myself.

"I want you more, I want... *us* more than I want this job."

Rune swallowed, his voice strained as he asked, "Now?"

I thought over the question. "No, not now. I'm too drunk to appreciate it fully."

"When?"

I tried to piece together my thoughts. "Tomorrow night?"

"Done."

"Wait!" I held out my hand for him to shake. He took it, his big hand engulfing mine.

"See?" I said, licking my lips. "It's now a deal."

"You'll forget this tomorrow."

"Definitely not," I informed him primly. "My body wants yours too much."

He groaned, dropping my hand to run both his through his hair. "You're killing me, Gabby."

I laughed, delighted. "Well, maybe I'll let you hear me through the wall again."

His eyes flashed, desire raw and desperate on his face. "Let's get you to the car."

CHAPTER 11

Rune

I saw Gabby through the glass door of the café, my body immediately clenching in response.

Maybe I'll let you hear me through the wall again.

Oh, she'd delivered on that threat. For over an hour last night, I'd listened like a sick fuck as Gabby had pleasured herself through the wall, telling me in graphic, filthy detail exactly what she was doing while I'd fisted my cock, desperate for her taste.

I'd never been this way about a woman before. Never thought about anyone with such a voracious intensity.

Now she was here, looking no worse for

last night, while I felt like ants were squirming under my skin, such was my need to
touch her.

I suddenly had a new appreciation for Jane Austen's wretched Captain Wentworth as he pined away for Anne.

You pierce my soul. I am half agony, half hope.

"Hey," she said, giving me a knowing little smile. "You look tired."

I moved to the coffee machine, giving her a single raised eyebrow in response. She had the good grace to blush.

"I'll bring your new books over tonight," I told her, my hands automatically moving to froth the milk.

A small smile played at the corners of her mouth.

"Only the books?"

I shrugged. "Did we make other plans?"

My cock felt heavy and hard, my body tight as I waited for her answer.

She accepted the offered coffee cup, her fingers brushing mine.

"I thought we had... an appointment."

I leaned over the counter, bending close to her ear. "Say it, babe."

"Your mouth on my pussy."

We both shuddered.

"If you want it, I'm more than willing to give it to you."

Gabby pulled back a fraction, her gaze catching mine, searching my face. "But do you want it?"

"More than you'll ever fucking know."

The gentle pink became a full flush. "Tonight then."

"Tonight."

The waiting was torture. Every moment of the day seemed to drag. I made mistake after mistake, until finally, I called it, leaving work at lunch.

The perks of being the boss.

Back at home, I didn't know what to do. I tried reading but found myself drifting. I went for a run but came home just as agitated. I showered then found myself out on the back deck, charcoal pencil in hand as I began to sketch.

From memory, I pulled up the image of Gabby on that first day. The curve of her lips as she smiled, aviators tangled in her hair. Long, graceful lines for her neck, shorter strokes for the turquoise encrusted choker that had wrapped around her throat.

I returned to her cheek, spending an obscene amount of time perfecting the curve of her smiling lips. I moved up, shaping her cheeks with shading, adjusting it just so to capture the beauty of her expressions. The tilt of one eyebrow, the shape of her eyes, the flare of her nose, each line required my full attention to ensure it was perfect. To ensure it was Gabby and not some poor imitation.

"Wow." Gabby's breath on the back of my neck finally broke the spell. "That's... I don't even know what to say to that."

I blinked, trying to refocus. I looked down at the drawing, casting a critical eye over it before looking back at Gabby, studying her.

It wasn't bad. But it didn't capture her spark. It didn't capture the way her eyes twinkled like she had some joke she wanted to share with you. Or the absent brush of hair from her face. It didn't capture how she constantly shifted from one leg to the other, the movement fluid and so subconscious it was like water.

"I should have realized you were an artist. Or should I say, *the* artist." She touched the edge of the heavy paper. "Are all the pieces and paintings in your house yours?"

"Most of them," I admitted, finding my voice was low and gruff as I stared at her, unable to tear my gaze from her beautiful face.

She smiled. "The sculptures at your shop?"

"Mine."

She nodded, her head tilting to one side as she looked at me. "You're a mystery I enjoy uncovering."

I laughed. "I have nothing to hide."

"Hm, maybe mystery isn't the right word." She raised one hand to her lips, tapping a finger against it. "Ah! A present. That's better. You're a present I enjoy unwrapping."

Desire ignited my blood, sparks leaping between us in the early afternoon light.

"Would you like to unwrap it now?" I asked.

Her eyes darkened, cheeks flushing as she nodded.

I put aside my equipment and reached for her hand, leading her to the door before pausing. "My bed or yours?"

"Mine," she whispered.

I nodded, stepping through. I led her to the bedroom, stopping in the middle of the room.

"You prepared for this."

The linen was turned down, the fan above us lazily pushing air through the warm room.

"Of course."

I turned to her, drawing her into me. "Gonna kiss you now, Gabby."

"Please do," she whispered as I cupped her cheek.

Yes.

My soul sighed at the first press of our lips. She was warm and wet, tasting of cream and spice. That first kiss unleashed something within in, flaming the desperate need I harbored for this woman.

You have bewitched me in body and soul.

"Fuck," I grunted against her lips as my arms crushed her to me. I had no pretty words in me for this moment, desire having burned away all restraint.

Her mouth opened under my lips, her body sinking into me as her tongue teased mine.

Fuck that.

I lifted her into my arms, turning us both before setting her on the bed and covering her with my body. My mouth was possessive and demanding as I took what I want, branding myself on her body. Under me, Gabby moaned, her body shifting as she let me lead.

I ran my hands over her body, grazing palms down her sides and then back up. Even as my body burned and everything in me roared to possess her, I put the brakes on, slowing it down, taking my time to build us both up. There was no hurry, no clock ticking in the background. There is only Gabby.

She placed a hand on my chest, pushing me back a few inches. Her lips pink and swollen, her eyes slightly glazed, her cheeks flushed.

I groaned, reaching down to kiss her again but she shook her head, stopping me.

"Let me take my leg off first."

I rolled off, propping myself up on the bed, watching as she reached down to begin removing the prosthetic.

"Can you... maybe not stare? Do something else," she said with a laugh. "You're freaking me out."

I grinned, deciding to tease her. "Like this?"

I shifted, reaching behind me to strip my shirt off. Her fingers faltered, hovering over her leg as her eyes raked my chest.

"I... haven't seen your chest before."

I'd been wearing a shirt the morning of Ferdinand's invasion.

"Considering we only just had our first kiss, I'm not surprised."

She groaned, hands covering her face, peeking out at me from between her fingers. "How are you a virgin?"

I chuckled, guiding my hands down my chest to rest on my fly. "Luck?"

She rolled her eyes, her hands moving quickly to remove the equipment then peeled the socks and sleeves from her leg.

"Seriously, look away, this isn't sexy."

"I don't know about that." I propped one hand behind my head, using the other to shove my jeans low on my hips, pulling my hard cock free. "I find everything about you sexy."

Gabby's eyes widened as she watched me lazily stroke my cock.

"What?" I asked innocently.

She licked her lips. "You're... umm... don't let this go to your head but... very big."

"And you're surprised?" I asked, cocking an eyebrow.

"Oh no. I mean, you did burst into my house to save me from Ferdinand with that monster waving about."

I grinned. "But?"

"But I just wasn't expecting it to look even *bigger*."

I couldn't deny the awe in her voice was doing fucking amazing things for my confidence.

"Hurry up," I ordered. "I wanna taste you."

She began to move, pulling off the final layers. "You've already tasted me."

"Not where I want to."

She shuddered, tossing the sleeve aside, looking at me.

"Done?" I asked, giving my cock another lazy stroke.

She nodded, licking her lips.

I reached for her, pulling her on top of me, enjoying her little squeal of surprise as I used her momentum to roll us both over, pressing her into the bed.

"Relax," I told her, enjoying how her breath caught every time I issued an order. "Let me explore."

I bent my head then hesitated. "If I do anything you don't like, let me know."

She nodded.

"Do I need to be careful of your leg?"

"No, but just a warning, I can't shave it." She ran a hand over her residual limb. "Ingrown hairs can rub and cause infections. It's probably a little hairy."

I cupped her knee, gliding my hand down to the end of her leg, circling the smooth skin before grazing back up. "Hair isn't a turn-off."

I kept up the gentle touch as Gabby lay back, and I started at her mouth, teasing her gently before deepening the kisses until our tongues were in a tangle and our lungs gasped desperately for air.

When her body arched under me, and her hands began to claw at my back, I shifted, drifting my lips across her beautiful face to her ear, biting gently on the lobe before sucking the sting away.

She whimpered but turned her head, allowing me greater access. I kissed and sucked my way down her neck, nibbling along her collarbone.

My hands dropped to the skirt of her summer dress, pausing. "You good if I take this off?"

She nodded, eyelids drifting open to find me watching her. "Please do."

I chuckled, pulling the dress up slowly as I continued to lay kisses along her neckline, my mouth practically watering for a taste of her breasts.

Her dress came off easily, leaving her in a pair of black lace underwear and a lace bra.

"Fuck," I swore, staring down at her. "You're gorgeous, Gabby."

She flushed, then reached for me, pulling me down to press a desperate kiss to my mouth before drawing back.

"Go, taste." She encouraged, pushing me down her body.

Thank Thor for decisive women.

I unclipped her bra, removing it from her body, revealing her breasts. Dark perfect nipples, breasts a generous handful, her body nothing but curves.

"You good there, virgin?" She laughed, watching me intently staring at her breasts.

"Fuck, yes."

CHAPTER 12

Gabby

I shivered – whole body shivered – at Rune's tone. His head dipped, his mouth closing over the nipple of my left breast.

"Oh God," I groaned, fingers burrowing into his hair, holding him to me. "Yes, like that."

He laved my nipple, his tongue decadently delicious against my sensitive body.

"Rune..." I arched under him, thrusting my breasts up as if I were a sacrifice. He made a satisfied noise in the back of his throat, a cross between a growl and a curse, the sound sending a responding quiver straight to my core. He looked up, his eyes flashing, raw desire on every line of his face before lowering his head to my right breast.

He paused, a whisper away from my nipple to grin up at me. I whimpered, then reached down, trying to find his glorious cock.

"Uh-uh. Don't distract me." He lowered his head, his mouth finding my breast.

I squirmed under him, desperate little noises escaping me. His free hand, the one not massaging my left breast, glided slowly up my ribcage, his hand came to rest against my throat.

Yes.

I closed my eyes, all my senses tuned to Rune.

"Fuck it."

My eyes snapped open as Rune abandoned my breasts, dropped to my pussy, shifting my legs wide to bend to my lips. His eyes met mine.

"I can't stand not knowing your taste."

His tongue. His nasty, filthy, gorgeous, beautiful tongue licked into me, continuing upwards, finding my clit.

"Fuck, Gabby. You're so wet, honey. You like this?"

I nodded, words escaping me as he teased my clit, his tongue and lips gentle but demanding. He looked so fucking satisfied as he tasted me. His gaze was dark and full of fire, and I found myself unable to look away.

"Come for me."

I moaned, my body shaking as his talented tongue teased every nerve ending.

A little more.

"Harder," I whispered, grateful when he responded, renewing his efforts.

A little—

"Rune!" My thighs clenched around his head, my body feeling as if it were breaking apart as I cried out, my body bowing with the force of my climax.

He swapped tongue for fingers, moving up the bed to press hot, gasping kisses to my skin even as he continued to play. His lips met mine, and I tasted me on his tongue, somehow finding myself more aroused by that than I'd even been.

"You ready?" he asked, guiding himself to me.

I hesitated. "I'm on the pill. And I'm clean."

"I never had a doubt."

I grinned. "Then come on, virgin-boy. Let's pop your cherry."

He kissed me, capturing my mouth fiercely, his teeth nipping at my lips, his tongue dancing against mine. I melted into him, my hips arching up, encouraging him to use me.

Rune surged forward, his thick cock working into me.

"Fuck." I flinched. He was big. Bigger than I'd expected, my disused muscles tight around him.

"Gabby?"

I looked up, giving him a small smile. "I'm good, you're just… rather large. You might need to work into me." I bit my lip. "How's it for you?"

"Valhalla."

I chuckled, my amusement shattering into naked desire as he shifted, gradually working his cock.

I groaned, hooking my thighs around his waist and pulling him tight to me. Without meaning to, my hips shifted, and we both hissed out a breath.

"Fuck, Gabby. Fuck. You're so tight." Perspiration dotted his skin, his body tense above mine. I buried my head in his neck, pressing tiny kisses there, listening to his labored breaths, as his pulse fluttered against my lips.

"Rune?"

"Yeah?" His voice sounded tight and strained.

"Fuck me."

He needed no further encouragement. Rune surged forward. This time we met in pleasure, our bodies working in tandem.

"Fuck," he groaned. "I'm close."

"It's okay." I panted. "I wasn't expecting—"

He cut my words off when he started to circle a thumb around my clit.

"Oh god, oh my god. Oh fuck. Oh, fuckity fuck. Rune, Rune, Rune." His name became a chant as he brutally fucked me, plundering my body, drawing from it exactly what he wanted.

My nails dug into his back, and with a slight twist of his thumb, he sent me over the edge once more, my body devastated.

Rune thrust twice more, then threw his head back, roaring his pleasure. He collapsed on me, his weight heavy but not overly suffocating. We lay panting, our hearts racing, for long minutes.

I tried to make sense of this moment. How I'd ended up here. Where it was going next.

You can't keep him.

I knew that. I'd planned to only have tonight. But after that, I knew tonight wouldn't be enough.

You're leaving.

I knew that too.

Protect your heart. You're not the family kind of girl.

I closed my eyes, mentally building a wall between us.

He propped himself up on an elbow, a

boyish grin on his face. "Please God, tell me that was good for you."

"Nah." I made a dismissive gesture. "Average."

He chuckled, pressing a kiss to my throat. "Liar."

I captured his face in my hands, committing his beautiful face to memory.

"It was perfect, Rune. Absolutely perfect."

"Good." He rolled, taking me with him until I was on top. "Now it's your turn."

I looked down, finding his cock was already hardening under me.

God bless newly ex-virgins. Their recovery time was inspiring.

"Oh, I think I can give you a little something." Even as I leaned down, my lips meeting his in a hungry kiss, I reminded myself that this wasn't for me. I wasn't that lucky. Unlike the romance novels he had me reading, there wouldn't be a happily ever after in my future.

Rune isn't for you. He never was. He never will be. You only have this moment.

And as much as I knew it would hurt, I was determined to wring all the memories from him.

I just hoped he'd forgive me when it came time to leave.

I cupped his jaw, pulling back a fraction, my gaze sliding over every inch of his beautiful face.

"You okay?" he asked quietly.

"Perfect."

He moved back in, pressing urgent hot kisses to my mouth as I filed this moment away, committing every detail to memory.

He's not for you. He never was. He never will be.

A single tear slipped free, falling down my cheek and onto the linen below.

Please remember me, Rune. Please don't hate me when this is over.

And with that wish of my heart, I pushed away all concerns for tomorrow and gave myself over to today.

CHAPTER 13

Rune

"Rune?"

I wasn't sure who was more insatiable – me or Gabby. We were at the point where we only had to glance at each other before our clothes were disappearing and I had her taste on my tongue.

I'd never thought of myself as an exhibitionist, but it was becoming increasingly clear to me that I would take this woman wherever and whenever she desired.

"Rune?"

That included on my fucking desk at work. I was meant to be scanning in a new book shipment, instead, I was staring at the spot where I'd laid her out last night, taking my time as I went down on her, teasing and taunting her hot body until she'd come, screaming my name.

"Rune!"

I snapped to, blinking at Ash. "Hey."

She laughed. "Hey space cadet. We're about to close up. That good with you?"

I glanced at my watch, frowning at the time.

Fuck. You've spent an hour daydreaming about Gabby. Get your head in the game, man!

I nodded. "Yep, let's do it."

It was parade day in Cape Hardgrave. All the businesses in town would be shutting early to head to Main Street for the kick-off of the fair. The parade would lead through the streets to the fairgrounds where the winning float would be announced, followed by the official opening of the fair.

Despite spending every free minute together – in bed and out – Gabby had been surprisingly tight-lipped about Thor's Shipbuilding's float. But then, I hadn't given her any hints about mine either. I'd even gone so far as to stash my costume in the office safe.

We closed up, heading to the storage shed down the block. I unlocked the roller door, revealing the beautiful longboat inside. It'd taken me and the team months of designing, crafting, and decorating but we were finally done.

"We're so winning this year," Ash declared, moving to loop arms with one of my other employees, Steven. The kid looked overwhelmed but not displeased with her attention.

"But does it work?" Natalie, one of the moms, asked. Her kid, Dee, was bobbing up and down, sucking nervously on her thumb as she looked up at the big ship.

"Does it work?" I scoffed, gesturing at them to grab an end. "Pull it into the lot and I'll show you."

We moved it out, revealing the ship's full glory. The mast was perfect, complete with a handcrafted sail, courtesy of Maisy and her grandmother, Mrs. Howell. The oars were positioned just so, and I'd handcrafted the dragon's head stempost myself.

But it was what dwelled at the bottom of the ship that I considered our pièce de résistance. Under the fake water, I'd installed a little smoke machine and battery pack. When turned on, the dragon's eyes lit, and smoke billowed from his nose and mouth.

I switched it on, tensing when nothing happened.

"Damn," Steve muttered.

"Give it a second," I told them, turning up the smoke level slightly. Wisps of white began to curl from the dragon's nostrils and my employees cheered.

"We're totally winning!"

Maisy and Mrs. Howell arrived a short time later, Maisy in her little Viking outfit, Mrs. Howell holding a shield for her.

"Thanks for doing this, Rune," she said as Maisy ran to join the other kids who were climbing over the float.

"Don't mention it. She knows most of the kids from Drag Queen story time, it made sense she should join in."

The kids were mostly those of my employees. But a few, like Maisy, attended some of the regular free programs I ran at work.

"We're ready!" Ash called from the stern. "All aboard, Captain!"

We quickly changed into our costumes, my employees chatting excitedly about winning the competition. I hooked the float up to the SUV, and Mrs. Howell gave me a wave, letting me know she was good to go.

"Slow and steady," I said to the team. "Ready when you are, Mrs. Howell."

"Roger!" She took off at a snail's pace, the float gliding gently behind. Even at such a slow speed, it took us no time at all to make it to the gathering area.

"Oh God." Beside me Ash snorted. "Rune... your family...."

I looked up from where I'd been breaking up a sword fight between two tiny Vikings to see the Thor's Shipbuilding float.

I shook my head, catching sight of my Nan nestled on the bow. I cupped my hands around my mouth, bellowing, "Nan! You traitor!"

In a buxom pirate wench outfit, complete with fake parrot on her shoulder, she gave me a bright wave. "Your brother asked first!"

Another point of contention – who Nan chose to align with each year.

"Next time you need a trip to the hairdresser, call someone else!"

I could hear her cackle over the bustle of the floats as the parade master assigned us numbers and directed us into position.

Ash sidled up to me, giving me a grin. "I slipped Bruce a fifty to put us in front of your brother."

I held up a hand, offering her a high-five. "This is why you're my favorite."

I hadn't seen Gabby, but I could see Erik and Laura at the front of the pirate ship, both with a twin dressed as either a tiny parrot or a monkey strapped to their chest.

My phone vibrated in my pocket.

GUNNAR

Rune... I'm sorry but...

I clicked the attached picture and shook my head. Liv, Astrid, Gunnar, and Ella were all dressed as pirates standing at the back of the boat.

RUNE

You're a disgrace to our family.

ELLA

If it makes you feel better, he's already ruined his costume.

She sent a picture of the giant tear down the back of Gunnar's pants.

LAURA

I hate to take sides but... we're totally winning this year. Sorry, Rune. We have a secret weapon.

I looked up but couldn't see anything unusual. The rest of the team from Thor's Shipbuilding had brought their families and were dressed as pirates. Even Ma and Dad were there, giving me a wave and laughing when they saw the longboat.

Just you wait.

The parade master stood at the front, lifting a megaphone to his mouth.

"Good afternoon everyone! I'm Bruce, the parade master. Welcome to this year's parade. Now, we're gonna take this nice and slow. Two full car lengths between each float. The lead float will set the pace. When we get to the end, look for me, I'll be the one in the hi-vis directing you to where to park. There're two awards – best in show and crowd favorite. Voting will take place directly after for an hour. The fairground will be open for food and drink. Once the mayor makes her speech, we'll announce the winner, open the fair, and rides will start. If you need help, call the number on your information pack. Otherwise see you at the finish line, good luck!"

With a cheer from the crowd, Bruce waved the first float through. It took a little while, but we were tenth in line.

"Hit it, Mrs. Howell."

She turned the music on, the soundtrack from the TV Series Vikings pumped out of the loudspeaker I'd installed in the back of the SUV. I bent, switching on our secret weapon, laughing when the smoke began to slowly wisp out of the dragon's nose, and all I heard were groans from behind me.

"Never fear! The dreaded Pirate Captain Gabby is here!"

I turned, and immediately knew we'd lost. Gabby stood at the front of the pirate ship dressed as a hot but entirely appropriately attired pirate queen – complete with authentic-looking peg leg. Beside her, stood Ferdinand, flapping his wings and looking ridiculously pleased when she fed him a small fish.

I heard cursing and groans behind me.

I shook my head, narrowing my eyes to give Gabby a death stare. She laughed, sending me a saucy wink before turning to the crowd we were beginning to near.

"Argh! Who be these sailors that we're about to plunder?"

Around me, our Viking kids threw chocolate coins into the crowd as we wound our way slowly down Main Street.

I was mostly preoccupied with making sure the kids didn't stab each other with their fake swords, but occasionally caught glimpses of Gabby, laughing with my family, ribbing the other guys from Thor's Shipbuilding, or balancing against the Mast and pulling off her leg to shake it at the audience.

I couldn't help but appreciate how seamlessly she fit. It was as if she'd always been here. As if she were meant to be a part of our family.

Admit it, you're fucked.

I knew she was still keeping distance between us. Despite my best efforts, I knew she still saw our relationship as a summer fling.

Well, fuck that.

My ancestors demanded more of me than allowing the woman I loved to slip through my fingers.

Brace, Gabby.

Little Miss Pirate Queen was about to get her heart pillaged.

CHAPTER 14

Gabby

I honestly couldn't remember the last time I'd had this much fun.

Or been this full.

I shoved the remaining ribs away from me, groaning as I patted my stomach. Beside me, Rune took a look at my plate, raising an eyebrow in question.

"Please," I said, shoving it at him. "I'm about to burst."

He took it, starting in on the remaining food.

"Legs like hollow trees, that one." Nan shook her head. "He'd eat us all out of house and home if we let him."

Rune rolled his eyes, but picked up a rib, tearing off a hunk of meat.

Why do I find that so arousing?

There was definitely something wrong with me.

"What do you think, Gabby?" Ella asked, leaning around Gunnar to give me a friendly smile.

"Sorry, about what?"

She gestured at the fair. "Starting something like this up back in the Cove."

"Oh." I swallowed, feeling Rune tense beside me. "I think it's a great idea. It'd not only be good for town morale but will bring in some fundraising for the emergency departments."

Ella nodded. "I figure if we approach Farrah—"

"Farrah?" Liv interrupted.

"The Mayor. She's the sister of my head chef, who also happens to be my best friend." She laughed. "It's nice to have a direct line to the top. Anyways, if we approach her, maybe she'd be willing to help set this up." She turned back to me. "You'd be willing to help too, right?"

I nodded, my stomach clenching at the idea of returning to Capricorn Cove. "Yeah, of course."

"Great."

From my other side, Ian stirred. "Will these women, Anika and Farrah be at your wedding?"

I saw Liv tense, her face wiped clean.

"Anika's my bridesmaid. And considering the whole town is invited, it wouldn't surprise me if the mayor makes an appearance," Ella said.

"They single?" Mac asked from across the table, earning a slap to the back of the head from Gunnar.

"Dude!"

"I said no fraternizing with the guests." He looked around the table. "And that goes for the rest of you cretins. I don't wanna have to deal with your bullshit on my wedding day."

Ella rolled her eyes. "Except if you're already together, like Rune and Gabby."

I choked on my drink, shooting a wide-eyed look at Rune. He ignored me, tearing off another rib.

"Um, we're not, that is... it's not quite like... that...?" I stuttered.

The table all looked at me, then Rune.

"Jesus," Astrid cried, shaking her head. "Rune, what did you do?"

"We actually like this one!" Liv said, reaching across the table to snatch at my hand. "She's wonderful."

"I already told you," Erik shook his head. "We've adopted her. You're kicked out of the family, buddy."

I looked around the table to see everyone glaring at Rune. He shot me a look as if to say, *see? And you were worried.*

I pushed up, suddenly overwhelmed.

"I... I have to..." The plastic white chair fell as I danced away from the table, needing to get away.

"Fuck, Rune! What did you do!"

"Go after her, dim wit!"

"Gabby, wait."

I heard Rune follow me, calling my name as I wove through the crowded eating area, desperate to escape.

I couldn't process my feelings right now. Rune was offering his love. His *family* were offering me their love. It was... too much.

I stumbled into the parking lot, tripping, feeling myself start to fall. Rune caught me, pulling me back against his hard chest.

"Gabby."

My name on his lips said in that warm, tender, heart-rendering loving way... it broke me. Tears flowed freely, my fingers an ineffective barrier. Rune growled, turning me around and pulling me back into his arms, tucking my head into his chest, holding me as I cried.

"I don't want to hurt," I sobbed, revealing my biggest fear. "I don't want to this to fail and then get discarded like every other time."

"Honey...." His arms were a tight vice around me, like chains binding us together. I should have felt trapped, but instead, it felt as if he were trying to tie me to him, keeping us connected despite the storm engulfing me.

As I calmed, Rune released me a little, just enough to look down at me.

"I'm about to lay some truth on you, Gabby. So, brace."

I tensed, waiting for the inevitable words to emerge from his mouth, my stomach clenching, bracing me for their impact.

"I want to marry you."

I blanched. "What!"

"Not right now. Maybe in a year or so. I know you need time. But I can't see my future without you. At first, I could. I'll be honest, falling in love with a non-reader?" His lips quirked. "It's a huge dealbreaker for me."

He brushed a stray tear from my cheek. "But then you kept appearing in my life, making it impossible to see or think of anyone but you. And yeah, I foisted books on you in hopes of you becoming a reader, but I suddenly found I didn't care that much. I found that I liked watching you. I liked your expressions and movement. I liked the way you joked with Maisy and teased my brother. I liked that you weren't afraid of my nephews, and bravely faced off Ferdinand."

I hiccupped a laugh, my heart thumping wildly in my chest.

"I love you, Gabby. It wasn't instantaneous but these past months have been the best of my life. I know you're committed to going back to the Cove, but, if you'll have me, I'll go with you."

"What about your store?"

He shrugged. "A store is cool and all, but it's not home. It's not my heart. You are."

I threw myself at him, wrapping my arms tight around his neck

"Are you sure?"

"Fuck yeah."

I raised up, kissing him with everything that was in me. He immediately took over, feasting on my mouth before breaking the kiss to press little nibbles to my jaw.

"I love you, Rune. Take me ho—"

"Ahem."

We froze, both of us twisting to look over at his shoulder at his family who were simultaneously watching us and attempting to look inconspicuous.

Rune sighed, stepping back slightly to sling an arm around my shoulder. "Make it quick."

Erik to me. "I know you're planning on going back to the Cove, but Mac has decided he'd prefer to stay with Gunnar and move to the Cover permanently. Which means Ian's about to get promoted and I'm gonna need another hand to help out." He gave me a grin. "You want the position?"

My heart thumped. "Gunnar?"

"Look, it's gonna be a loss. But I figure, what I lose in an employee I'll gain in a sister-in-law."

I looked up at Rune, my heart in my eyes. "And what say you, Sir? Should I stay?"

His grin was slow but brilliant. "Fuck. Yes."

I turned back to Erik. "I guess it's a yes."

At my words, Rune swept me up, throwing me over his shoulder, headed for his truck. His family called out ribald suggestions as he headed out, flipping them the bird over his shoulder.

My phone vibrated in my pocket. I squirmed, pulling it carefully free.

*LIV HAS ADDED GABBY TO
LARSSON FAMILY CHAT*
ASTRID

Welcome sis!

ELLA

Get ready for the crazy.

GUNNAR

Don't tell her that, you'll scare
her off.

ERIK

She's gotta be prepared.
Besides, this is Rune we're
talking about. She probably
already knows.

LIV

Don't listen to them. We're all
perfectly sane.

LAURA

I don't know. You remember the
rat incident, right?

ELLA

Or the time Gunnar moved to
Capricorn Cove after knowing
me less than a month?

GUNNAR

Hey! You make it sound like I
didn't decide to do that within
three seconds of meeting you.

Laughing, I tucked the phone back in my pocket as Rune carried me to his car.

This must be what being in a family feels like.

CHAPTER 15

Rune

I wasn't gonna make it to the house.

I knew this, my fear at losing Gabby, my relief at her agreement to stay, my overwhelming anger at her for building a wall between us instead of talking to me, it all exploded, searing through my veins, wiping every thought from my head except one – mark her.

I whipped into the parking lot at The Literary Academy, throwing the truck in park and jumping out. I ran around to the other side, throwing open her door and lifting her out once again, tossing her over my shoulder.

"Rune!"

"Quiet," I ordered, charging toward the staff entrance. "I'm this close to fucking you against the brick wall right now. You say one word and that restraint is gonna break."

She was quiet for a moment while I fiddled with the key, cursing when I couldn't find the right one.

"I'm okay with a fuck against the wall... if that's what you need."

The little control I had shattered, splintering reason, and logic. I set her down, backing her up until her back pressed against the brick of the wall. We were in the alley between The Literary Academy and a furniture store next door. The alley was sheltered from the view of the main street, and both stores were closed for the day.

But that didn't mean there wasn't a chance of getting caught.

Mine.

"Turn around," I ordered, my hands dropping to my belt. "Hands against the wall, spread your legs."

Gabby stared at me for a moment then turned, moving far too slowly for my liking, the rage still fizzing through my blood.

I pressed into her back nipping at her neck, sucking her ear lobe. She groaned, arching up, her spine bending back to try and grant me better access to her neck.

"You're never fucking leaving me, Gabby," I told her, unzipping her pants and roughly shoving them down her legs. "Never. You got me?"

She nodded but it wasn't enough for the fear still running through my veins.

"Say it!"

"I'm yours. I'm never leaving."

"Again," I demanded, rising up to rub the head of my cock against her clit.

"I'm yours," she whimpered, her hips jerking as my cock collected her slick, spreading it to better tease her sensitive skin.

"I'm yours, Rune!"

I slammed my cock into her, brutally punishing us both. She cried out, pressing back against me, her body bowing as she tried to take me. I worked into her tight little snatch, marking her, branding her, desperate to fuck this need out of my system.

"You're mine, Gabby. We're a fucking family. You and me, babe. You and fucking me. No more running. No more walls. Nothing but this." I thrust harder, my hands holding her hips in place.

"Yes, oh my god, yes."

I nipped her neck then sucked the sting away, ensuring I left a mark.

"You're gonna come for me, Gabby. You're gonna fucking milk my cock and take my load then you're gonna say thank you and tell me again you love me. Got it?"

She nodded, now incapable of words as her body jerked with the motion of my thrusts.

I reached around, my fingers finding her clit. I found a rhythm I knew would drive her crazy, my fingers knowing just where to press.

"Now," I ordered, tweaking her clit. Her pussy gripped me in a vice, her body bowing, nothing but gasps leaving her lips as she came.

I followed, my cum branding her.

Mine.

She dropped but I caught her, pressing her close, holding her tight, nuzzling her neck gently as we both came down.

"Rune?"

I winced, wondering if I'd taken this too far.

"Yeah?"

She sighed, looking up at me with dreamy eyes. "Let's do that again."

Any leftover tension dissipated, leaving me feeling a little like a wet rag.

"How about we get cleaned up first. Then I'm gonna take you in our bed."

Her lips lifted; the smile so heartbreakingly

beautiful that my fingers itched for canvas to capture it.

She reached up, pressing a kiss to my mouth. "I love you Rune, please, take me to our home."

Her every wish would always be my command.

EPILOGUE ONE

Gabby

"No."

"But—"

"I said, no. Abso-fucking-lutely not."

I hid a grin, pretending to flip through the bridal magazine that Liv had brought over.

"Look, as Gabby's Maid of Honor –"

"Excuse me?" Astrid interrupted from the kitchen, placing hands on her hips. "Who the fuck decided this?"

I chanced a glance at Rune catching him mid-eye roll.

"Ladies, if we can get back to the issue at hand—"

"I did," Liv answered Astrid. "You get to be mine."

"What if I don't wanna be yours?"

Liv frowned. "Why the ever hell would you not want to be my Maid of Honor?"

Astrid held up a hand, marking off the reasons on her fingers. "One, you're a crazy control freak. Two, you're totally gonna be a bridezilla. Three, you're not even dating let alone engaged. Four—"

"What about the guy from Ella's wedding?" I asked. "I thought you liked him."

Liv waved us both off. "It didn't work out."

"Probably cause you're too controlling..." Astrid muttered.

Liv ignored her, turning to Rune. "Brother, I get it, you're possessive. But I'm telling you right now, there *will* be strippers."

"No, there won't."

"Yes, there will."

"Do you remember Ella's bachelorette?" my future husband asked. "Do you remember the police being called? Do you remember Ian having to bail you out of jail?"

Astrid snorted, caught Rune's glare then ducked her head, suddenly very interested in lace samples.

"Look." Liv made a placating gesture at Rune. "We've learned our lesson; I'm not going to allow that to happen again."

"Yes, because there won't *be* any strippers."

Her mouth twisted into a benign smile. "Of course, Brother."

He frowned. "I mean it, Liv. If I hear of one goddamned man in a G-string—"

"I said, okay." She turned to me. "Now, dresses."

I shrugged. "I still think an elopement would be fine."

"It's getting more attractive every day," Rune muttered.

"Absolutely not," Liv declared. She handed a dress folder to me. "Now, do you want white, eggshell white, ivory, champagne, oyster, cream, blush, or..."

Hours later we finally bid farewell to the maids from hell.

"We really should just elope," I told Rune for the hundredth time that day. "We can live stream the ceremony from Fiji.

"Yeah, good luck sneaking that one past Liv. I'm pretty sure Ma gave her authority to place a tracker on our bank accounts. They even get a whiff of us purchasing a ticket they'd be here, stopping our escape." He shot me a grin. "They're determined to welcome you into this family properly."

Too late.

In the year since Rune and I had been together, his family had been nothing but wonderful. His sisters had welcomed me with open arms, slowly changing every photo on my wall from those of strangers to images that included me, surrounded by his family.

The best decision I'd ever made had been trusting Rune with my heart.

The second-best decision had been attending the Greedy Readers Book Club and getting drunk enough to confess my desire to Rune.

God bless book club.

Rune pulled me into his arms, pressing a kiss to my forehead. "You okay with this?"

I looked up at him, cupping his jaw. "Your family can be overwhelming, but this is good. I'm glad they're so excited."

"Don't let them railroad you."

I grinned. "Only your Nan can do that."

He chuckled. "I love you, Gabby."

"I love you too."

"You wanna act out that scene from The King's Horrible Bride, tonight?"

I laughed. "You mean the one that got me all hot the other night?"

"Mm." He ran hands down my back, cupping my ass. "There's something so fucking attractive about a woman who reads."

"Well, Mr. Librarian. Perhaps you should get me between the covers."

He chuckled. "Yes, Ma'am, right away."

EPILOGUE TWO

Gabby

I tiptoed down the hall, pausing at the door to our daughter's room.

"And then the princess declared that she didn't need a prince to complete her, but that she loved him anyway, and so they lived happily ever after. The end."

I rolled my eyes chuckling quietly to myself.

"Daddy?"

"Yes, baby girl?"

"When I grow up can I marry a princess?"

God love my husband; he didn't even pause.

"Of course, sweetie. You can marry

whoever you want." He paused then, and I waited knowing a caveat was on its way. "Except a politician. I'm sorry, baby. No matter how much I love you I just can't allow that kind of negativity into our house."

"Okay, Daddy."

I heard him kiss her then walk across the floorboards to stand at the door. "Now, straight to sleep, munchkin."

"Love you times a million!"

"And I love you times a million. Night."

He switched off the light, softly pulling the door halfway closed, blocking the light from the hall.

"Hey," I whispered looking pointedly at my watch. "She was meant to be down a half hour ago."

"And you weren't meant to be home until ten."

"I skipped out early."

We met half-way, Rune wrapping arms around me, me tucking hands into the back of his jean pockets.

"Everything okay?" he asked, searching my face.

I nodded, breathing in his familiar scent. "Just missed you."

"Oh really?" He pressed into me, letting me feel the hard outline of his cock.

"And maybe that," I admitted, flushing.

This month's book club had been discussing Kresley Cole's Game Maker series. I *may* have gotten a little worked up talking about my favorite scene.

"Daddy?" Our daughter called from her room. "Can I have a water?"

Rune sighed, shaking his head. "She's definitely yours."

He twisted, calling over his shoulder. "No. You already had a drink and went to the toilet and got a second story. Go to sleep, Tora!"

"Okay."

We both stood still for a long moment, trying to suppress our giggles. When we were sure she was down and staying that way, we crept back down the hall to the living room, Rune pulling me onto the couch and across his lap.

"Here?" I asked as he settled me over his erection.

"Anywhere," he grunted, hands sliding up my thighs to find my bare skin. "Jesus, Gabby. Where's your underwear?"

"I took them off when I got home. Complaining?"

"Fuck no."

Rune lifted up, turned, then gently placed

me back on the couch before dropping to his knees and disappearing under my skirt.

"Quiet," he ordered against my core, his breath hot on my sensitive skin. "Don't wanna wake her up."

I bit the inside of my cheek as he pressed slow, druggy kisses to my thighs, my abdomen, my lips. He parted me, his fingers sliding through my slick wet, teasing at first, then becoming faster, the pressure increasing as he fed my need, building up my climax.

"Rune...."

"Shh..." he admonished. "We don't want to wake Tora."

I reached for a throw pillow, pressing it against my face as he replaced his fingers with his mouth, his tongue finding my clit, tasting me, circling in the way that he knew was guaranteed to drive me crazy.

It came like a freight train, my body clenching, arching, grasping for more.

"In me," I ordered, throwing the pillow aside. "Now!"

Rune surged up, almost lifting my skirt over my head in his haste to cover my body with his, guiding his cock into me, thrusting hard and deep. I wrapped my legs around his waist, the angle causing us both to groan.

Even after all this time he constantly rocked my world.

"Quiet," he reminded me, one hand coming up to cover my lips. "Or I'll have to fill this filthy little mouth."

I moaned against his palm, remembering the last book club night when he'd done just that. Remembering how he'd tasted as he'd come down my throat.

My body clenched around him, my pussy milking his cock as that memory crashed into this moment, pushing me over the edge. I came, biting his palm as my world exploded, Rune buried deep in me.

"Fuck yes, Gabby. Come around my cock. That's it, milk me, honey."

I felt his thrusts increase in tempo, his cock pulsing as he came deep, hot cum warming my inside.

Rune collapsed on top of me, breathing heavily.

"Wow," I whispered some time later.

Rune chuckled. "You can say that again."

We got up, me moving to our bedroom to clean up, Rune moving to close down the house. We met on the bed.

I was rolling on my compression sock when he came in, standing at the end of the bed, clothed only in boxer briefs.

"Again?" I asked, eyeing his rapidly hardening cock.

"Mm, seems I can't get enough of you tonight."

This time was slow and sensual, hours of foreplay and touching, of kissing and tasting before Rune rolled over, his hands gripping my waist to support me as I rode him to completion.

"Love you, Gabby."

I snuggled into him, pressing a kiss to his heart. "Love you too, Rune."

We were quiet for a moment, the house silent around us.

"Gabby?"

"Mm?"

"The agent got back to me today. They want to option our comic."

I pushed up, leaning across the bed to stare at him. "Are you serious?"

He grinned, his teeth flashing in the dark. "Yeah."

Two years ago, Rune and I had worked on a comic book together. I'd been pregnant and terrified our baby would be born without a limb.

Not because I was worried she wouldn't be whole, or wouldn't be loved – I had no fear on that end. No, I was worried that she wouldn't have good role models to look up to. No superheroes or comic characters or fictional princesses that she could point to and say, "they're like me."

Rune, in his infinite wisdom, had suggested we write our own. I developed the storyline; he drew the images. We'd called it *The Last Librarian*, and it'd featured a woman who saved the world – and just happened to be a wheelchair user.

"This is amazing news! Think of all the kids that'll get to see Frankie." I pulled him close, kissing his beautiful lips. "Rune, this is...."

"I know." He gave me a tight squeeze.

I laid my head on his shoulder. "We make a pretty good team."

"No, babe. We make the best *family*."

My heart smiled.

Yeah, we do.

———

Thank you so much for reading The X-List! I hope you fell in love with Rune and Gabby.

Desperate for more Rune and Gabby?

Check out EvieMitchell.com for your bonus extra!

Next up is Reality Check, featuring Liv, who is in a bit of a pickle thanks to a certain red-headed Sasquatch.
Curl up with Reality Check NOW!

ABOUT THE AUTHOR

Hey, I'm Evie Mitchell.
I'm a thirty-something romance author (she/her/hers) living with disability. I believe in inclusion, accessibility, and fierce romance. My loves include steamy romance novels, my sexy husband, our THREE sausage dogs (THE FUR!!!), and my ever-growing collection of book-related mugs.

As a woman with a diverse work history, including in areas such as hospitality, retail, emergency response, event management, human rights, disability access, and security— my books are filled with true stories (bridezillas), worst-case scenarios (malfunctioning zippers), and my favorite tropes (one-bed).

I'm a strong proponent of #OwnVoices, and specialize in fiercely inclusive happily ever afters.

As You Wish
You Sleigh Me
Meat Load
Resolution Revolution

Dogg Pack
Puppy Love
Bad English
The Frock Up
Pier Pressure
Trick or Trent
New Year's Faye

Reigning Hearts
The Marriage Claim
Silent Knight

Men of Trinity Bay
Kink in the Road

Nameless Souls MC
Runner
Wrath
Ghost
Shield

Elliot Security

Rough Edge

Bleeding Edge